The Hunt

Mila Crawford

Created with Vellum

Author Notes

Dear Reader,

This novella contains content that could be disturbing to some readers, please read at your own risk.

-Somnoph!l!@, Degrad@tion, Prim@l Play, Praise, Sp!t pl@y, Breath Play, Dubcon, TVP, DP, MMMF, Cream Pies, Impact play, Crawling, Angel Wings. Asphyxiophilia.

-Play with sharp objects used to cut up fruits, and vegetables.

-Play with red bodily fluid

-Religious Masoch!sm

-Religious Trauma

-CSA (not on page)

-CA (Not on page)

-Child neglect (Not on page)

-Torture (Not FMC)

-Violence and violent acts (On page)

-Self-harm (On page)

-Mention of suicide

-Death of a parent

Chapter 1

Lorne

She's feeding the chipmunk. Just sitting there on the lawn, hand out, offering her lunch to the tiny rodent. What is that type of kindness like, to care about life's smallest creatures?

I glance around her. Not another soul in sight. For a girl who's nice to everyone and everything, she sure lacks friends. You'd think all the vultures on campus would flock to her. The perfect con, too sweet to believe the world is full of bastards who would [illegible] chew her up and then spit her out.

"What are you looking at?" Cas asks.

"Perfection."

Cas nods. He has his back to her. He never looks at her in front of me, but I've caught him staring. He returns his attention to his phone, pretending to have something important to focus on. "She's a do-gooder. She can't handle us."

I bark out a laugh. "How would you know unless you've been watching her?"

Cas turns his gaze on me. "We fuck together. You want to fuck her. So I did my research."

"I don't want to fuck her."

"Is that why we haven't banged a chick in months?"

I glare at Cas. We've been fucking together for years. It's the only way it works—the two of us and a chick. But since I first set eyes on her, I can't seem to think of anyone else. Cas wants to say this whole situation is on me, but he hasn't floated a name either.

It didn't start out that way. I only wanted to check her out and get the lay of the land. She was going to be an integral part of my life, after all—someone I'd see regularly. But then curiosity turned into something else—obsession. That's why we're here at the university. We're not students, but we harbor an insatiable need to learn all we can about Noelle White.

Pieces of drywall fall onto the floor as my fist creates a hole in the wall. My knuckles are red and raw, but I don't care. I need the distraction. Violence is Cas's coping mechanism, but it also seems to work for me. When in Rome, I guess.

I don't know what it is about this girl. She probably doesn't even know what a cock looks like, let alone what to do with one. But whenever I close my eyes, I see her on her knees with her hands wrapped around our cocks, begging us to choke her.

I gaze up from my hand and watch as Cas stares out the window in her direction. "She'd look hot covered in cum."

"I fuckin' knew it. You want her too."

Cas shrugs. "I like to fuck. She has three holes." He squints, hands balled into fists, jaw tight.

"What is it?"

"Who's the fucker?"

I jump toward the window, my eyes narrowing. There, beside our pretty little Snow is Peter, the fuckin' khaki-wearing loser. She's smiling up at him. They talk for a minute, and then she pats the grass beside her, offering him a place to sit.

My stomach turns. She's never once offered me a smile like the one she's giving him. Maybe in a different life, if I were a better guy, she would have. “I think his name is Peter. He’s a senator's son. I’ll dig up some information.”

“Or we could just smash his brains in.”

I turn to Cas. He’s grinning, but his eyes are void of life. It’s the same look he gets when he takes care of loose ends. That’s why he’s so good at his job. He has no empathy, no remorse, and no tangible emotion. At least the psycho is loyal. “You can’t kill him on campus.”

“No problem,” he says, his grin growing larger. “I can do it when he’s off campus. I want to use that new hacksaw. Oh, I also got a new drill. The thing is powerful. I’m sure I could take an eyeball out in five seconds.”

“We have business dealings here, Cas. We don’t shit where we eat.”

Chapter 2

Caspian

I'm gonna cut off his dick and feed it to him. It's only fitting since that's probably why he's talking to her. His eyes will be next. Gonna pop them right out of his colossal head. Maybe play hacky sack with them. I only need to cut out one eye to do that, so he can watch me play.

"She's smiling at him. Why is she smiling at him? That guy can't be funny. Look at him."

Lo[illegible]e slaps my back as he laughs. "Thought she [illegible] just another pussy."

"She is. Our pussy, and I don't like people touching my toys. Especially new ones."

"Jesus, Cas, stop."

I turn to look at Lorne, but my vision is blurry. "We're gonna kill him, right?"

Lorne pulls a white cloth from his pocket and dabs it on my face.

"What the fuck are you doing?"

"You broke the glass with your head, Cas. You're bleeding."

I turn to the window. Shards of glass are now on the pane and the floor around my feet. I didn't even realize I'd done it. I tend to zone out when I get angry. The only signs of what happens when I do are apparent on my flesh. But usually, it's someone else's blood.

"What the fuck was that, man?"

Ignoring Lorne, I stare out the broken window at her. I want to beat the grass she's sitting on because it's touching her ass. Then I see it; his hand on her leg. Fucker thinks he can do that without losing a limb. "He. Is. Touching. Her."

I take the stairs two at a time, almost flying until I get to the door. Pushing it open, I stomp to where she's sitting in the yard. "Get the fuck away from her, and I'll make it hurt less when I kill you."

"Who the fuck are you?" the punk demands.

His stupid face has a shit-eating grin. Before I can say anything, Snow places her hand on his and turns to look at me. I make a mental note to break the hand she's touching first.

She beams at me, and I swear it's like being bathed in the warmth of the damn sun. "Hello."

"Hi. Tell him to get lost."

"Why would I do that? I'm having a conversation with Peter, who's a perfectly nice guy. You, on the other hand, should go to the hospital to tend to your wounds. You have a gash on your face, and blood is staining that glorious Good Vibrations shirt."

I love her. She knows who the Beach Boys are. I'm torn between bending her over and fucking her until she calls me Daddy or killing the piece of shit who's still touching my girl.

I'll make Peter cry like a little bitch before I put him out of his misery. I don't like that she's being nice to him. She shouldn't be nice to anyone other than Lorne and me. She looks so pretty as she tries to hide her anger, but I can see her teeth grinding as she holds a fake smile. It's not her usual smile. This one is tight. Her dark eyes widen as I loom over her.

"Get up. We're leaving."

Her expression quickly moves from anger to shock. I'm not sure if Sunshine can be angry, but her pretty eyes narrow at me, and her full lips form a straight line. Something weird tugs inside me, something foreign and confusing. I don't like how she makes me feel. It's probably because I haven't fucked her. If I fuck her, she'll be out of my system, and life can return to normal.

But she likes the Beach Boys.

"You don't want me to force you to get up, Sunshine. I'm not known for being gentle."

"Cas, I've never spoken to you a day in my entire life. Usually, when someone wants to talk to me, they say hello like Peter over here and engage in an actual conversation. This caveman nutjob thing you have going on won't work."

Her breath hitches as my hands wrap around her biceps and hoist her into my arms.

The little preppy weasel jumps to his feet and steps toward me. I bark a laugh. "It's cute that you're pretending to be a man when you're so scared you want to piss your pants."

"Get your hands off her," he demands, his body shaking.

"Who's going to make me? You?"

Pain shoots up my arm. I look down to see her teeth digging into my flesh like a piece of steak.

I ignore her love bite and stare the preppy fucker down. His eyes move from her mouth on my arm to my face, and his hands leave streaks along his Khaki pants. Buddy is sweating, but he's still willing to try to protect her. I like that about him. He's not a total douche. Maybe his death will be quick.

"Let her go."

"Aw, look at him, Sunshine. He doesn't realize he's a Teacup Poodle going up against a Pitbull."

Chapter 3

Noelle

The metallic taste of blood fills my mouth, but I don't let go. Cas has his arm wrapped around me. He's huge. Maybe he takes steroids. I'm a size eighteen, but I'm a particle of dust compared to him. I don't think I've ever felt this small beside a man. I'm worried about Peter, who's trying to stand up to Cas. I'm sure he could beat Peter to a pulp while holding me with one arm.

What is that digging into my back? Something hard is poking me, and I move my arm behind me to check it out. Oh, Cas is aroused. How is he getting hard from me biting the shit out of him? He's crazy. Certifiable.

"Let her go, Cas," a deep voice I recognize comes from behind us. Lorne Miller. It makes sense he'd be close by. These two are always together. Cas, and there's another guy, Declan.

They don't go to school here, so I have no idea why they think they can get all up in my business. They appeared a few months back. At first, I assumed my father had decided to have them be my shadows after Lorne kept showing up at our house. But my father assured me that wasn't the case and said Lorne probably had his own business to adhere to on campus.

But it's not just Lorne. It's always him and his shadows. It's almost like they're Lorne's personal bodyguards. Very inappropriate bodyguards, according to the girls' bathroom. Celia Warren mentioned she caught them hooking up a few months back. She then proceeded to tell us how they only have sex with girls together. Which I guess makes sense since neither has ever been seen with a girl without the other around.

It's not like they couldn't get any girl they wanted. They're incredibly attractive in different ways.

Lorne is the type of guy who could charm any protective father. He's clean cut, well put together, and walks around with an air of intelligence and superiority.

He's tall. I'd say slightly over six feet. His medium brown hair falls effortlessly and would be the envy of many girls if it was long. He's not as huge as Cas. Lorne's muscles are lean and cut, much like an Olympic swimmer. But what makes Lorne stand out are his beautiful piercing green eyes that would make a cat jealous.

Cas has the whole bad-boy vibe. He's always dressed in black to match his raven hair and the tattoos that peek through the collar of his band t-shirts and on his arms. Today he's wearing a Beach Boys shirt. Can't hate a guy who appreciates Brian Wilson, one of the greatest musical revolutionaries of the twenty-first century. He's wearing ripped black jeans, and although they probably cost five-hundred dollars, they don't look pretentious on him. As for Cas, he wears them like an iconic badass, giving James Dean a run for his money. I glance at his black motorcycle boots. Shit kickers.

Cas is a beast. He's almost two feet taller than me and towers over my five-two frame. His arms are like sculpted boulders, and his eyes ... an icy blue that makes you feel you're about to be possessed by the devil. It's also evident he's not all there.

"She looks like she's about to take a chunk of flesh out of your arm."

"I know. It made me hard," Cas replies gruffly.

A shadow falls over me as Lorne faces Cas. "You're gonna spook her."

Too late, Lorne. Cas is clearly a psycho.

"I don't care. That little fucker touched her."

"Peter, I think it's time for you to scamper off," Lorne says.

Scamper? Who says that?

"I'm not going anywhere until I know she's safe," Peter says, his voice lacking conviction.

I let go of Cas's arm. "I'll go with you, but you have to promise you won't hurt him."

Cas shakes his head. "Can't do that."

I kick Cas in the shin with the heel of my boot. Cas groans, but it doesn't sound like he's in pain. What the fuck is wrong with him? "He didn't do anything."

"He looked at you. He's lucky his eyeballs are still in his head."

I stand there dumbfounded, glaring at Cas. My death stare doesn't have the desired effect because he simply grins at me like a nutjob who just won the lottery.

"Please, Lorne. Do something," I beg.

"It's not up to me. Peter here isn't moving his feet along."

I gaze at Peter, defeated. I'm small and unsure and at the mercy of the brute holding me back. "Peter, please, go."

"I'm not leaving you with these two," he says stubbornly. "Her father will bury you if you hurt her."

I freeze. Peter knows who my dad is. It's no secret that my father is a powerful man. A man who snaps his fingers and the world shifts to his will. Edward White is a man you don't mess with because he will crush you. The only person he listened to was my mother. She tethered him to the ground, but that ended two years ago when she finally lost her long battle with cancer. I miss her. I miss the color and vibrance she injected into my life when we were surrounded by darkness.

Now it makes sense why Peter is here pretending to save me from the big, bad wolves. He's trying to show that he's worthy, that he's not a coward, even as he shakes with every word he utters. I recognize men like

Peter—powerless and willing to do anything for the tiniest bit of control.

This is about his ego, not my safety. I'm so stupid. He isn't interested in getting to know me. He's interested in the daughter of Edward White. I'm the key to the kingdom, and anyone who wants to meet the king can't be a good person.

Guys like Peter are all the same. Relationships are commodities to them. It's about what looks good on paper, what gets them the best deal, and what creates envy. I shouldn't care what happens to him, but I can't help it. I care because I'm not my father. Because I believe in compassion and mercy.

Chapter 4

Lorne

Perfect Peter, the son of a senator, knows who her father is. Isn't that interesting? Edward White and I move in the same circles. He was a friend of my old man's before he died. He helped me learn the ropes when I took over the business at eighteen. Probably too young to dive feet-first into a life of crime. Edward has a lot of connections in high places, and it looks like this little weasel knows it.

Peter thinks Noelle is his "in." Little does he realize Edward would happily eat his lunch while he watched one of his men snap Peter's neck.

"I'm losing my patience, Peter." I glance at him, noting his shaking hands despite his smirk. "I suggest you put your tail between your legs and scamper off."

I pull out a pack of smokes and put one in my mouth, lighting it with my zippo. Peter remains silent, his eyes wide as I take a pull of my cigarette.

"Do you know who my father is?" he demands.

There it is. The little boy can't stand on his own feet and needs daddy's name to make an impact. "Your father is no match for me."

Peter folds his arms and smiles. It's a "gotcha" smile, like he knows something I don't. "And you're no match for her father."

I take another drag of the cigarette, stepping close to him and blowing the smoke in his smug face. "I'm confident her father will thank us for taking care of the little boy who tried to violate his daughter."

Uncertainty clouds his eyes. That's the thing with little punks whose balls haven't dropped yet. They want to play with the big boys but can't handle the heat. It's cute how they swipe and show their teeth in defiance, but in reality, they're cubs in a den of rabid wolves.

Silence surrounds us like a dense winter fog. This world is seeped in corruption, danger, and manipulation. It's hard to see if you're unaccustomed to it. Peter is playing "dress up," a little boy attempting to do a man's work.

I take another drag of my cigarette as if I don't have a care in the world, which I don't when it comes to him. But I can't have Cas killing him in broad daylight with witnesses. "So, what's it gonna be, Peter? Will you live another day, or will you be meeting the Grim Reaper?"

Peter glances from me to Noelle. She's tense but no longer trying to fight off Cas. Her hands are balled into fists at her sides, and her pretty mouth looks fucking delectable covered in Cas's blood.

"Tell him you're fine, Noelle," I order.

She glances at the sky as if asking heaven for support and guidance. Her chest rises and falls as she takes a deep breath before her eyes land on mine. She looks tired; maybe it's sadness. Her pretty dark irises appear haunted, like she's not with us. I want to know what she's thinking and what she hopes the outcome will be. My heart squeezes as I see a lonely tear roll down her soft cheek.

"I'm fine, Peter. Just go."

Peter steps toward her, and Cas growls.

"Peter, I suggest you don't get too close," I advise. "Cas doesn't have a good handle on his emotions."

Peter nods once and walks away, his head down and his shoulders slumped. Even now, he's pretending he gives a shit about her, but the only thing he cares about is his golden ticket with his daddy.

"You can let me go now, Cas. He's gone," Noelle says, wriggling to free herself. "Can't you control your dick?"

"Not when you keep moving up and down against it. This is your fault."

"If you let go, the problem will be solved."

Her elbow connects with Cas's solar plexus, and he moves back. She leaps away from him, adjusting her hair without taking her eyes off Cas, who's staggering toward her.

I glance around the yard. No one has paid attention to what happened here. That's usually how it goes for us; people know we're here but are too scared to acknowledge us.

Noelle turns to me, her eyes seething with anger. She doesn't say a word. She doesn't have to. For the first time in my life, I'm ashamed. Not because of what Cas and I did or for running little Peter off. I'm ashamed because there's nothing I won't do to claim her.

Noelle thinks she can handle us, but her mother never prepared her for the monsters in our world. She never told Noelle about the two standing beside her with hungry eyes devouring their prey.

"Stay away from me. Both of you," she says firmly before turning and walking away.

"She has a mean elbow," Cas says as he stands beside me, and we watch her sexy ass stomp across campus. "I'm not staying away from her."

"You can't stay away from something that belongs to you. Little Snow doesn't know it yet, but she's claimed."

Chapter 5

Declan

"We're going to that party tonight," Lorne says as he tosses himself on the wingback chair in my room.

I turn to Cas, standing beside the St. Andrews cross, his fingers gliding along the shelf, which holds a variety of whips and floggers. "This room is so creepy. Ever think of modernizing it?"

"That's rich coming from you. Don't you get off on draining blood?"

Cas grabs one of the whips off the shelf and snaps it. Shame floods me when I get hard watching him. He glances at my crotch before meeting my eyes. He smirks and cracks the whip again. Little fucker.

"Take off your clothes, Declan. I'll even let you come," he taunts.

I turn away from him, and my gaze lands on my black bedspread.

"You want to be nailed to the cross. Play your whole Jesus shtick?"

"Fuck you," I whisper so softly I'm not even sure I said the words.

The bed shifts and Lorne grips the nape of my neck, yanking my head back. His intense green eyes bore into mine. "Leave him alone, Cas,"

I grasp Lorne's sides and wrestle him on the bed before straddling him. His hand falls from my neck.

"There he is," Lorne murmurs.

My breathing is heavy as my eyes bore into his. That's always been our thing—I drift into the past, and Lorne pulls me back to the now. I wrap my fingers around his wrists and raise his arms above his head, crushing my mouth to his. The kiss is hard, needy, and desperate.

I've only ever kissed Lorne. I've never felt safe enough with anyone else. I fuck Cas, but I won't kiss him. There's a wildness about him that scares me because I'm frightened my demons will rear their heads. I teeter on the edge of insanity, but Cas is already there. He has no remorse or pity. He runs on hedonistic needs, and for someone like me, that's a recipe for disaster.

I almost kissed a girl once, but the darkness came, and I nearly strangled her. I'm attracted to women, but they trigger me. Women send me back to a place of darkness that I'm constantly trying to outrun.

Movement on the bed. A tap on my cheek.

"No way I'm being left out," Cas says with a smirk.

I break the kiss, turning my head to see his thick cock.

"Open up, boys."

That's Cas's thing; having two mouths on his dick. I'm sure if all he got were blow jobs for the rest of his life, he would be as happy as a pig in shit.

I roll my eyes and part my lips for him as he shoves his cock inside. His hands move through my hair, pulling the strands as he slides his cock in and out of my mouth. "Such a good cock sucker."

Cas pulls himself out of my mouth, trailing saliva that Lorne wipes on his hand.

Lorne tugs my joggers below my ass and pulls out my dick. He moves his hand, now lubricated with my spit, up and down my rock-hard length. "You ready to fuck me like a good boy?"

I nod, unable to form words. Sometimes I'm the aggressor, the one who bends one of them over and rails their ass until I feel better. But I don't want to think right now. I don't want to lead tonight. I want to be told what to do.

"Give him the lube," Lorne demands.

Cas leans back and opens the nightstand drawer, grabbing the lube and tossing it to me.

Lorne's intense gaze holds mine. "Take off my pants."

My hands shake as I fidget with his black leather belt, sliding it through loops. Cas's eyes light up as I hand it to him.

My trembling fingers pull down Lorne's pants. He lifts his legs, not allowing me to take off his shirt.

I pour the lube, which glistens on his balls before trickling to his asshole. Lorne hisses as I work in the lubricant. "You ready to get fucked, Lorne? To be taken like a little bitch?"

Lorne nods.

"Tell me. Tell me you're my little bitch and want me to fuck this tight little ass until it's full of my cum."

Lorne cocks an eyebrow. "You talk a big game. Let's see if you can finish the task."

I turn to Cas, who's wrapped the belt around one hand while the other strokes his cock. "Remember, my shoulders only."

Cas nods before slapping Lorne's face with his cock. He slips his cock into Lorne's mouth as I thrust mine into his ass. All three of us groan in unison.

"Fuck," Cas moans. "I'm not sure who has a better mouth, you or this cocksucker."

I spit, and my saliva falls on Lorne's hard, twitching dick. I use my thumb to move the spit up to the head and apply pressure.

Lorne lifts his ass as I fist his throbbing dick in my hand. "Cas, do it."

The first sting of the belt lands on my back. It's always better with Cas. He doesn't show mercy like Lorne, who likes to give pleasure. But Cas was born in sorrow. For him, pain is pleasure. Like me, he enjoys inflicting and receiving both.

Lorne's hand roams up my body as Cas wields the belt along my shoulder blades. The blows get harder with each thrust of my cock in Lorne's tight ass. Cas pops his dick out of Lorne's mouth, lost in his aggressive handling of the belt.

Lorne's smile is twisted. This is when he lets the mask drop and shows us the darkness he holds deep within. "What's better, Declan, praying to God or fucking like the devil?"

I hate him for doing this to me, but I also love him. I have the same emotions about God and the church. I've spent my entire life in purgatory, one foot in heaven and the other in hell. The need for bliss and agony are so tightly entwined that I'm not sure one would survive without the other.

My muscles tense. The hate I have for them, and myself rages like a storm that swiftly becomes a tornado. The poisonous vines of desire tangle around my heart and mind, clouding my clarity. It's always like this. My body crumbles to lust, and I abandon the hereafter for a moment of pleasure.

I grip Lorne's throat with my free hand and dig my fingers into his flesh. I unleash every ounce of rage I have for myself on him. He opens his mouth, and I spit inside. I want to debase him for what he makes me do, what he makes me crave.

My heart constricts with pure love for him and Cas. Logic unravels, reminding me that they don't make me do anything. It's me who's evil, who desires the pleasures of the flesh more than the divine.

"Be a good boy and lift your legs, Lorne," I instruct.

Lorne smiles, and the dim lighting makes his green eyes appear demonic. He holds the back of his knees and moves his legs so his feet almost touch his head.

Cas shoves his cock deep into Lorne's mouth as I tighten my grip on his throat. Gagging noises and the crack of the belt hitting my back echo around the room.

"Harder, Cas."

The lashes of the whip soothe me, a penance for my lack of self-control.

Chapter 6

Caspian

"Harder," Declan gasps.

Between fucking Lorne's tight ass and the slashes from the belt, the dude is losing his mind. I'm not going easy on him, but he wants more. I pull my arm back and wail on him.

For a moment, I contemplate stopping. As much as this shit gets me off, for Declan, it's more than simply blowing his load. It's about suffering because his cock is hard, and he's fucking Lorne's ass. Declan's pleasure always comes with immense torture in mind and body. But every time I hear the belt slice against his back, my cock twitches in Lorne's mouth.

I grip Lorne's head and push my dick to the back of his throat. I glance at his hand. He's not moving it, so the fucker can take more. That's what we watch for, his hand tapping against his thigh. It's crazy that he allows two murderers to suffocate him, especially as I'm a murderer who gets off on the killing part. Lorne gets off on not breathing and takes breath play to a fucking whole new level. But then again, I like some fucked up shit myself.

"Dec," I groan. I'm close, but I can't cum, not without it.

Dec nods. "Do it."

I abandon Lorne's head and pull at Dec's neck until my teeth graze his skin. Then I bite down. My eyes roll to the back of my head as the flavor of Declan's blood floods my mouth and triggers my orgasm. My cum drains from my cock into Lorne's eager mouth.

"Fuck," I grunt as I pull out of Lorne's mouth. "Didn't realize it had been so long since I unloaded."

"That would explain why you only lasted five minutes." Lorne chuckles.

Fucking prick. I shake my cock above his face, and a few more drops of cum coat his face. "You look like a good little bitch, covered in my jizz."

Lorne raises an eyebrow. "Make that mouth of yours useful and give Dec a hand."

Fucking asshole. "You know, motherfucker, you talk too damn much." I shove my hand on his face, covering his nose and mouth. I turn to Declan. "Pay attention to his hand."

Dec glides Lorne's dick in my mouth. My tongue swirls around the head before I force my head down, taking him to the hilt.

A strong hand comes to rest on top of my head. "That's it, Cas. All the way down. Show us what a big man you are and how well you take a nine-inch cock down your throat."

My lips are restricted around his girth, and I know it's not worth saying shit cause it will come out as muffled moans. The little shit. Next time, I'm going to strap Dec on the St. Andrew's cross and go to town on him, so the fucker won't even be able to lie down.

He always gets like this after he comes. It's like he hates everyone and everything because of what he did. Some fucked up shit with his childhood. It's why he only watches while we bang girls, never joining in.

He seems to think if he doesn't fuck them, he's staying pure somehow. He also treats the girls like shit. The only time he ever takes part is to spank or cane them, trying to justify why he got turned on watching her getting railed. Almost like if he punishes her, he absolves himself. I usually bust another nut while I watch him because the marks he leaves on their skin are a fucking work of art. Better than any porn.

Lorne's cock twitches in my mouth, and he cums in long waves. *Fuck.* Apparently, he hasn't busted a nut in a while too. I close my lips firmly around him, letting him pump everything he's got into my mouth.

He gasps as soon as I let go of his face, his breathing shallow. "Fuck. Cumming is way better when you think you're about to die."

I move off his dick and turn to him with a cum filled mouth. Slapping his face, I bring my lips to his and kiss him, allowing the cum to pass from my mouth to his. "Might as well eat your cum, asshole. You need to fuckin' whack off more. That was like a fucking fire hose."

Lorne shoves me off him, resting on his elbows, all of us standing there with limp dicks. "Shower and get dressed. We're going to that party tonight."

Dec moves off Lorne, scrambling to get his pants on. He always hurries to get dressed, as if he didn't just fuck us. He thinks he can deny it ever happened if he gets his clothes back on quickly. It's annoying as fuck. One minute he's with us, getting into fucked up shit and having a good time; the next, he's back to his goddamn preacher-boy nonsense.

The words burst out. "You're a fucking killer. You think your God is fine with that, but not fucking?"

Declan won't look at me. His fucking eyes focused on the ground. "I repent for it all."

I rummage through my pants, pull out a joint, and walk up to him, my semi-erect dick still hanging out. This motherfucker. I grab his cock, my grip tightening as he tries to worm away. He flinches and turns away as if he didn't just come in Lorne's ass. I bring my mouth close to his. "Good enough to fuck but not kiss, huh? That's okay, Dec. I'm used to people using me. My father did it, so why the fuck not you?"

My hand drops from his dick. I stare at him, waiting for him to say something. After a minute, I storm out of the room with my cock still hanging out, leaving my pants on his bedroom floor.

CHAPTER 7

Noelle

I hate parties. I especially hate frat parties full of entitled rich boys who think the world should bend over and cater to their every demand. I never come to these things but my best friend, Briar, dragged me out. Briar's a different breed than me. If she's oil, I'm water. Our friendship shouldn't make sense. We shouldn't work, but we've been inseparable our whole lives.

She's good with people, and she's comfortable around them. The only time I speak to someone when I recognize kinship. Most people make my palms sweaty and my head spin. It's hard to decipher if they genuinely like me or want something from me. Part and parcel of being my father's child. That's why I spend most of my time outside in the woods or sitting on a couch reading a book. It's safe—no mind games or quick words trying to get one step ahead.

Briar sighs as she grabs my hands. "Can you stop fidgeting with your dress? You look beautiful."

I smile at her, even though I think her statement is ridiculous. She put me in this short little black dress not made for a girl with a size forty-two G breasts. A classic, she called it. My boobs are about to burst out and flash everyone. And it's so short that I can't bend over without showing everyone the goods. Briar's definition of classic and mine are not the same.

I scan the room. "I feel like everyone's staring at me, picturing me naked. I don't want anyone to see me naked."

In the corner, shrouded by darkness, I see a group of guys ogling me. They look like their eyeballs may pop out of their heads. "Look at those guys over there. They're checking me out like a pack of wolves salivating over a cut of Kobe beef."

Briar giggles. "I think wolves would be more into rabbits. How would they know what Kobe beef is?

I swat her arm, joining in with her laughter. "Oh, you know what I mean."

"If they're looking at you like you're Kobe, that means you're doing something right. There isn't much better than Kobe beef."

I grab her hand, pulling her away from the prying wolf eyes. "I don't want to be looked at like anything. I don't wanna be Kobe beef, tenderloin, or ribeye. I definitely don't want to be a fucking rabbit. Why couldn't I wear my jeans and a blue sweater?"

Briar rips her hand out of my grasp. "Because you need to have a little fun, and your normal clothes don't scream fun. They scream, 'I'm a virgin who's going to die with a million cats."

"Well, the virgin part isn't true. I lost it to Jimmy Fitzpatrick during my senior year of high school."

"One time, Noelle. You slept with a guy one time. Obviously, he didn't know what he was doing because your pussy has grown cobwebs since then from the lack of use. Let loose. Have a little fun."

"I don't think your idea of fun is the same as mine," I grumble.

It's true Briar and I are not the same. She likes men and embraces her sexuality. She's a woman who knows what she wants and never gets attached, breaking hearts and leaving broken men behind in her wake. Briar is a man whisperer. The crusher of the coldest heart.

"Let's get you a drink. Maybe that will loosen you up."

"Or maybe you shouldn't drink because it can get you into trouble, especially in a room full of wolves waiting to devour you," I mutter beneath my breath.

"I heard that," Briar says as we walk through the crowded room, holding each other's hands.

She drags us into the kitchen. It's the most crowded space in the entire house, which is ironic because you wouldn't assume a bunch of frat boys and half-drunk sorority girls would be interested in hanging out in the kitchen. This isn't like the kitchen parties my grandmother described to me as a child, where she and her friends gathered around talking about their annoying husbands and obnoxious children.

Briar delves into a giant round tin bucket and fishes out two beers. "Here." She thrusts one toward me. "Have a few of these. It'll help you chill out."

My hands shake as I remove the twist top and tip the bottle to my lips, taking a swig. At first, it's sweet, but then the bitter flavor of alcohol takes over my taste buds. I've never been a fan of booze. I'd rather curl up on the couch with a big mug of hot chocolate and lose myself in the fictional world of a good book.

"Briar Rose. Little miss sleeping beauty herself." The voice belongs to Malachi Frost, a creep who's been chasing Briar all year. "Why don't you bring your pretty little ass over here where my buddies and I are. I promise we'll show you a good time."

Briar glances at me. I'm not sure if she's asking permission, if she wants me to get her out of the invitation, or if she's inviting me to join her in beating the shit out of Malachi.

"I don't know. I'm with my friend. It wouldn't be right for me to abandon her."

"I'll keep Noelle company."

"That's so nice of you, Peter," Briar says, turning to me. "Is it okay if you hang out with Peter for a while so I can have a chat with Malachi?"

I'm not a fan of Peter's, but he's relatively safe. The guy isn't gonna overstep when he wants me for my connections to my father. I'm pretty sure he realizes that if he tries anything funny, my father won't be too keen on taking any meetings from him.

I wave Briar off. "Yes, but please be careful."

Briar blows me an air kiss. "You're the best."

"And for the love of God, please watch your drink. I don't care who these guys are, you can't trust them!" I yell after her.

Chapter 8

Lorne

"He's not coming," Declan says.

His hands are buried in his pockets as he shuffles his feet back and forth. He didn't want to come tonight. He wanted to stay in his room and beat the shit out of himself for being who he is.

"Can you blame him? He loves you, Declan, and you love him. The sooner you admit that to yourself, the easier our lives will be." I take another drag on my cigarette before tossing it on the ground and crushing it underneath my Italian leather boot.

"It's not the love I have a problem admitting."

I know, but his problem is like the elephant in the room: none of us know how to address it or fix it. So we do what we know; sex and violence.

I clap my hand on his back and shrug. "We're all a little fucked up, man. Rejection is hard for him."

Declan gazes up at the sky, refusing to meet my eyes. He's focused on a dark cloud, or maybe the moon, some fragments of a fatherly figure he never had and always desperately wanted.

"Nothing's up there, Dec. Your entire life, they've made you believe in an invisible man in the sky who's going to bring you a reward or subjugate you in hell-fire. It's all a fucking lie. Every single ounce of it. A fabrication created to gain control."

"We've all got our coping mechanisms. Mine's hope."

"The thing about hope is that it's not something someone can give you. Hope is something only you can give yourself."

"Well, look at you getting all philosophical." Cas appears with a shit-eating grin.

I don't know what's happened in the last two hours that's made him do a complete one-eighty. He went from a melancholy asshole who sat up in his room playing metal versions of some Patsy Cline song on his guitar to pretending the moment in Declan's room never happened.

"I'm glad you made it, brother."

He pulls out a joint from his pocket and lights it, taking a long haul. His eyes fall on Declan, "There's not much a good fuck, great music, a night ride on a motorcycle"—he holds up the joint—"and one of these bad boys can't fix."

"So you're good," I ask.

"What's there not to be good about?" Cas takes one more drag of his joint before putting it on the ground with his boot. "Now, let's get in there and fuck some pussy."

Declan stops in his tracks. "Is that why you brought me here? To go chase some tail?"

I walk past the groups huddled on the front porch and into the frat house. Body after body crowds the area. The place is a human sardine can. The smell of alcohol, sweat, cum, and female arousal hits my nostrils like a punch in the face. In every corner of the room, people are trying to get off.

"Not precisely!" I yell behind me to Declan. "We're here to make sure no one touches our property."

Cas pushes through the crowd, moving in front of me. “Wet pussy that I’m getting in tonight, one way or another.”

I sigh in frustration. Cas’s ego is going to get the better of him and fuck us all. “We’re not getting in her one way or another. We don’t fuck girls who say no.”

Cas grins at me, pulling out a little baggie of white dust from his pocket. “I’ve got party favors.”

“What the fuck is that?” I ask.

“Sleeping pills. Put a little in her drink. Fuck, she’d look so hot asleep. I mean, I wouldn’t put my dick in her cunt or anything, but I wouldn’t mind cumming on that sweet pussy and taking a few snapshots for the spank bank.”

“Let’s find her first.”

Cas doesn’t seem to hear me as he takes the steps two at a time.

“Why the fuck are you running upstairs? Cas, we don’t have time for this shit.”

Cas turns to me with the same rage-filled expression he had on campus the day we saw her with that little motherfucker. “I saw Peter take her upstairs. And she didn’t look like she could stand on her own two feet. That motherfucker gave her something.”

I don't let Cas finish the sentence. I push past him and fly up the stairs. I hear Declan and Cas's frantic footsteps behind me. Cas doesn't need to worry about Peter because if he touches even a hair on her head, I'll rip him apart, limb from limb. I warned that motherfucker not to go near her again, and I always follow through with my warnings.

Chapter 9

Declan

I'm not one of those people who sees beauty in the world. All I know is ugliness, pain, and sadness. I was born in hell. I was raised in fire. And I deal in retribution. But every day, I repent in the hope of salvation.

My life is about avoiding temptation. I'm a flawed man. I stumble daily. But as I gaze at the two people I love most in the world, I have a moment of peace before her voice echoes violently in my mind.

If a man lies with a male as with a woman, they have committed an abomination; they shall surely be put to death; their blood is upon them.

And that's when it all crumbles into ash. I can no longer look at them as two people I love. All I see are serpents of hell tempting me into the world of sin. Not only am I disgusted with myself, but I'm also disgusted with them.

Some days I think they'd be better off if I left, and they'd never have to see me again. They could be happy, but I'm too selfish for that because they're the only two people who've made me feel like I'm not the spawn of Satan and I'm worthy of love.

Lorne bursts into the room first. I've never seen him so out of control. He's the one with the level head. He's cool, calculated, and void of emotion. Well, that's what people think when they don't know him. Iceman. But he enters the room like he's about to explode, and that's a rarity. It's a side you only see if he gives a fuck about you.

The Peter guy looks shocked. His eyes scan between the three of us and the door, trying to find an escape route. His hands are by his side, and his fingers twitch nervously.

"Get the fuck away from her," Lorne growls.

Peter's face is priceless. The guy looks like he's been caught with his pants down. I suppose he would have been if we'd arrived ten minutes later. He raises his hands in the air, trying to feign innocence. "She was tired, man. I brought her up here so she could lie down. I swear I was going to leave."

He's nailed his coffin closed. We haven't said anything, and he's spun a tale. That's what guilty people do—assume you knew their intentions and try to convince you that wasn't their plan. Well, Peter, I hope you've made peace with your maker because you're about to meet the grim reaper.

Cas's arm flies through the air, landing directly on Peter's face. Blood splatters from his nose, and he stumbles back. "Real smart, motherfucker. Leaving a fucking drunk, defenseless girl alone in some random dude's bedroom at a frat house. Like frat boys are fucking Catholic choir boys. What do you think would happen to her if one of these drunk douchebags walked in and saw her?"

Cas isn't thinking rationally. He wants a reason to beat him. Peter will probably be dead by morning, but Cas is doing what Cas does best—playing with his food before he devours it whole. I think it comes from the shit his father made him do.

Regret fills my gut as I remember his expression earlier. I hate that I hurt him, but he's trying to get something from someone who's broken. Broken people can't heal anyone because all we're trying to do is survive.

Peter opens his mouth, but Cas punches him again before he can speak. "That was a rhetorical question, asshole. I don't need you to open your big fat mouth and tell me more lies. We warned you to stay away from our girl. We told you what would happen to you if you didn't. Who the fuck do you think you're messing with?"

Cas is on the ground on top of Peter, his fists flying mercilessly. Confusion rises within me as I watch Cas unloading on the guy. He has no issues with violence. Of the three of us, he thrives on it the most, but this is out of control for him.

Cas likes to make a production before he kills someone, much like a serial killer. He sets the scene, makes a few jokes, and uses creative methods to inflict torture. But this is raw, pure emotion projected into his violence. This isn't about a job or revenge. The violence within Cas is solely about his feelings. Cas cares about little, except Lorne and me. Growing up the way he did, he's only ever wanted a family—something the two of us share in a diverse, twisted way.

My gaze moves to the bed and the vision lying on top of a cum-stained comforter. A manifestation formed by the devil to smite me and cast me straight to the depths of hell. My own personal Eve.

I hear her voice again, like an unwanted message played on repeat.

But each person is tempted when lured and enticed by desire. Desire, when conceived, gives birth to sin, and sin, when fully grown, brings forth death.

"Cas, stop. We've got other shit to deal with," Lorne says.

His voice is a little too cold, a little too low, too calm. Lorne is the opposite of Cas. He's just as crazy, but his derangement comes from a different place.

Cas doesn't give a fuck and will do whatever he wants when he wants. His actions are based on his hedonistic needs and enjoyment.

Lorne is calculated. Every move he makes is methodically thought out and planned. I fall somewhere in the middle, unable to control my needs and desires. Regretful of my choices after I make them, to where my brain is bludgeoned with a monsoon of remorse. Yet I never learn from my mistakes and commit the same ones over and over again. That's my purgatory.

"Who's the girl?" I ask, unconcerned about Cas's homicidal tendencies on Peter and Lorne's desire to make it end. All I can focus on is the dark-haired raven with crimson lips and a body designed by the devil himself to entice the most pious of men.

She's wearing a short black dress that's risen to the bottom of her pussy. Her thick, shapely thighs are slightly parted, giving me a perfect view of her virginal white cotton panties. I'm convinced she's a jezebel because she's done something a girl has never done. She's made my mouth water and my cock throb with need.

"Someone Peter shouldn't have messed with," Lorne says, snapping me out of the trance she put me in. Lorne hauls Cas off Peter and places his hands on the sides of his face. "You can't kill him yet."

"What do you mean, yet?" Peter slurs. Cas must have broken his Jaw. "I'm pressing charges. He's an animal. He should be locked up."

Lorne turns on Peter, his movements quick and lethal as he slams him against the wall by his throat. "You fucking fool. Do you know who I am? You think Cas is an animal? I'm the king of the jungle who controls all the beasts, little boy. Imagine what I can do to you with the snap of my fingers. Now, here's what you're gonna do. You're going to run along and tell your daddy some random person mugged you. You couldn't make out a face since he was wearing a mask. Then you'll go to bed and rock your stupid ass to sleep. Once you are asleep, you'll have nightmares, and it'll be my face you see. Do you understand me?"

Peter nods as wetness forms at his crotch and a stream of piss puddles on the floor. "Yes. Yes."

Lorne releases him. "Clean up your mess before you go."

Lorne laughs as Peter looks at him in confusion. "You're not my puppy, Peter, and you certainly aren't the little dog of the owner of this disgusting room. You made a mess, so it's only appropriate for you to clean it.

Peter nods. "Oh, okay. Let me get a cloth."

Lorne laughs. "Why, Peter? You have a perfectly good tongue. Get to work."

Peter falls to his knees, his hands on either side of the puddle of urine. He stares up at Lorne in a final silent plea, begging him not to have to go through with such a humiliating act.

Lorne shakes his head. "There's no forgiveness here, only damnation."

Peter's pink tongue falls out, and the first licks of urine glide from the floor into his mouth.

Lorne kicks his foot underneath Peter's chin, directing his head. "Think you missed a spot, Peter.

All of it."

Peter gags as he cleans up the rest of his piss from a floor that looks like it hasn't been cleaned for the past year.

A snicker. My eyes land back on Cas. He's holding a joint and leaning against the door frame, smirking like a Cheshire cat while he witnesses Peter's humiliation. I know this isn't the end of it.

"Good boy, Peter," Lorne says in a condescending tone, like a grandmother speaking to her little dog. "Now, get the fuck out of here."

"I get to kill him, right," Cas asks as he blows out circles, creating a smoky haze in the room.

"Follow him. Make sure he does as he's told."

Cas stomps his feet. "I get to kill him, right?"

"Yes, Cas, you get to kill him. I just wanna make sure you're not stupid about it."

My gaze shifts back to the curvaceous beauty. "What are we gonna do with her?"

Lorne sighs as he lights a cigarette and approaches the temptress. The red ember from the tip of his cigarette glows like a flame as he takes a drag and glides one finger along the sleeping girl's lips. "We're gonna get her out of our system."

Chapter 10

Lorne

I've never seen Declan so much as glance at a woman before. He's always there when Cas and I fuck a girl. He gets off on it, and sometimes he'll fuck Cas or me or ask one of us to fuck him while he watches the other fuck the girl.

But he never touches the woman.

He's got some fucked up thing about women. We thought it was taken care of when we killed his aunt, but it was so deeply embedded in him, he's suffered his entire life. Declan hates women. He thinks they're the personification of evil and that nothing good can come from falling in love with one. It's fucked up, considering how religious he is, and the point of most religions is to procreate and multiply. But Declan has some deep-seated trauma caused by a woman who was supposed to protect him.

The first word he learned was "Devil," with a finger pointed at him. And that was after being traumatized by a junkie mother who would sell him to the highest bidder for the thinnest crack rock or a hit of heroin.

I take a drag of my cigarette and stare at him. He's not standing by the door anymore. He's now at the side of the bed, looking at the girl. Her tits are exposed, and her dress has ridden high on her thighs.

That fucker was about to fucking do something to her. I realize how fucked up it is because Declan is touching her the same way Peter would have, and I don't care. Because, unlike Peter, we don't want her for any reason other than we crave her.

Declan's touch on her skin is right. It even seems divine. I never claimed to be a fucking good guy with morals. I'm just a guy who will do anything I fucking want and protect those I love and those who are mine. Little Snow doesn't know she's ours, but she will soon enough. She's the queen of our hellscape, the center of the trinity. The earth that grounds us.

"Burn the memory of her body in your mind through touch. This is what the pearly gates will look like. She's the path to paradise."

I expect Declan to tell me no. That there are some sins he won't commit. But to my shock, he brushes the tip of his index finger along her hard nipple. Fuck, the girls got the hottest tits I've ever seen, with the prettiest pink nipple on top like the perfect cherry on a Sundae. So huge that I want to be smothered by them,

I step away from the wall toward Declan. I press my hand against his dick bulging in his pants as I grind my growing erection into his ass. "You hard, Dec? Because my cock is about to bust out of my pants watching you touch her. Pull up her dress, Dec. She's sleeping. It's the perfect time. Take a bite of the apple, Declan, and be free. Be like God. Know every pleasure and experience every sin."

Declan's breath hitches, and he leans into my chest.

"Don't worry, Dec," I say as I unbuckle his pants and pull out his belt. "I'll always give you what you need."

My hands fumble along the collar of his black dress shirt as I pull it off his shoulders, exposing his scarred and tattered back. Years of whips, belts, and canes have left him covered in scar tissue, all beginning at the ripe old age of three.

I hiss and turn away, not wanting to witness the years of trauma he wears upon his flesh. I long to go back to the day when we killed the bitch who started it all, hoping to break the cycle of his past and help my friend be free. "Go on, Declan. Touch her pussy."

Declan keeps one hand on her breast, squeezing it gently. His other hand roams down her body and over her tempting curves until he reaches the hem of her little black dress. "She's beautiful, Lorne. She looks like an angel, and all I wanna do is violate her."

He lifts her dress as I unbuckle his pants. His cock unleashes onto my open palm. "I don't want to use the belt, Declan. I want to be buried deep in your ass while you tongue fuck her. You're going to eat that sweet cunt while I rail your ass. You're not going to cum, Declan. Know why?"

"No," he pants.

"Because I'm not willing to punish you for it. I'm tired of dealing with your need for penance. So instead of whips and belts stinging your back, I'm not going to let you cum."

He pulls her panties down to her ankles and over her feet. Then he brings his face to her cunt with an audible inhale. I push his face into her pussy and hold it there while yanking his pants down.

Commando.

I slip my hand into my pocket and take out the small bottle of lube, squirting it in the crack of his ass. "Eat her out, Declan. Get high on her and forget about God." I rub my cock with the silky liquid before pushing into his ass.

Declan moans between slurps. God, she must have a juicy fucking cunt.

I pull Dec off her and kiss him, overwhelmed by a ravenous need to have her flavor on my tongue. "She tastes good, Dec. She's going to be sitting on the table for us with her legs spread so we can have a little taste whenever we want. She's the one, Declan. The key. She's who you need because it hasn't been Cas or me."

"I need," he croaks

My heart cracks. I'm aware of what he's asking of me. His eyes are sullen and sad. He's like the sad kid I met in my first year of high school.

I press my lips to his again as my cock moves in and out of him in slow torturous movements. "Do what you want with her, Declan. She'll give you what you need. If she doesn't, we'll help you."

Relief floods his face as he smiles, and he nods before moving back to Noelle's pussy.

"Blessed isn't the man who endures temptation. Blessed is the man who succumbs to desire. If God didn't want us to fuck, suck, and lick, he wouldn't have made it feel so good."

Declan wails as he pushes his ass back, trying to get more friction with my cock.

"Why do people scream for Jesus or God when they're about to come?" I fuck him hard, railing his ass with no mercy. "Church doesn't lead you to heaven. It's my dick in your ass and your tongue on her pussy that does."

I snake my hand around Declan, gripping his cock. "You like this, Dec. Your cock has never been this hard before. You want to fuck her, don't you?"

"Yes," Declan cries.

I understand that admission took a lot out of him. I'm shocked that he's even doing this. When Cas and I banged other girls, Dec sat in the corner and jerked off. I'm pretty sure he wasn't jerking off over the woman but over our treatment of her. That was something we did for him. He needed to watch us degrade them. Probably some fucked up shit with his past.

I grip the back of his neck and push. Declan thrashes under my hand. I know he's having a hard time breathing, but I don't care. I'm close, and I need this.

Usually, Cas chokes me so I don't harm anyone else, but he's not here, and this will have to do.

"It's a baptism, Declan, and her cunt juice is holy fucking water."

I pound into him until I can't take it anymore. I pull out of him and yank his head off her by his hair, pushing him aside as I fist my cock and release my cum all over her pussy. Branding her with my scent, marking her as mine.

I turn to Declan. "You want to lick my cum off her, don't you?"

He hesitates, watching my cum glide down her slit.

All I can think about is our cum oozing out of her three holes. I grab his hand and pull him toward me. "We're going to do this together."

On our knees, our faces an inch away from her hot, wet cunt, we part our lips and clean her pussy with our tongues. It's erotic, tasting our depravity and consuming our lust.

"Fuck," Declan moans. His eyes fall closed. He's in the moment.

This is when he's with me, when he doesn't think about how he should punish himself before the man in the sky does.

I grip the back of his neck and tilt his head back. His mouth opens wide, and I spit my cum inside, admiring how it rests on his tongue. "Give it back to me, Dec. Fuck the blood of Christ. This is the sacrament."

Declan's eyes open. The look of peace vanishes, and I see the lurking sense of panic, feel it creeping into his flesh. He's not in the moment anymore. His body is rigid. His hands shoot up.

I'm on the ground in a flash, his hands pressing on my throat. I can't breathe. My cock rises. I want to fuck and be fucked. I crave it. My mouth opens, but the pressure of his hands makes it impossible for me to speak. He spits the cum in my mouth. I get lost in the sensation of running out of oxygen and the flavors flooding my mouth.

"You want to corrupt me, Lorne. You want me to be depraved like you. Like Cas. To have no remorse?"

He moves his body on top of mine, his hard cock moving closer to my mouth. "You want a communion, Lorne. I'll make you drown with the heavenly father's love."

Chapter 11

Declan

Rage builds within me as my fingers push against Lorne's throat. "Foxes have dens, and birds have nests, but the Son of God has no place to lay his head. But your mouth is a good place for his cock."

Lorne's face has turned red from the pressure of my hands, and my cock lodged in his throat. My head falls back as power surges through my veins, holding his life force in my hands. "The great Lorne Miller. Nothing but my little fuck toy. What would happen if you died right now? What would you say to your maker? Would you beg forgiveness or demand to burn in hell? "

I push up to my knees and pull out of his mouth. He gasps for breath as soon as I release his throat. But his rock-hard cock tells me he's enjoying every moment of this.

His emerald eyes lock with mine and he smiles. Spit froths at his lips and trickles down the sides of his mouth. "If loving you will banish me to hell, I'd burn for all eternity."

His words enrage me because they wound me more than anything else anyone can do to me. I can handle the physical torture the man offers, but I cannot handle his compassion. I don't deserve it.

I push my cock back into his mouth and mount him, my hands back on his throat, my abs smothering his face. His hands tap my side, but I don't move. I pound into his warm mouth with my eyes closed as I try to escape anything that lies heavy on my heart or mind. For once, I want to forget the torment raging in my soul.

My dick jerks as my body stiffens. I groan as my cum sprays out of my cock into his mouth. He sputters as cum and saliva spill from his lips and land on the stained carpet.

Shock rocks me as I realize what I've done. I lost control. I succumbed to the darkness that whispers to me. She referred to me as the spawn of Satan, and that's exactly what I am. There was no fall for me because I was the seed of evil planted into innocence.

I jump off Lorne, not wanting to be in the presence of his warmth any longer. I don't deserve love. I don't deserve grace. I don't deserve loyalty. "Don't fucking tell me that shit again. Because next time, I *will* kill you."

Lorne's laugh is a wheeze. "You think that's a threat? I like to hang myself and jerk off."

"How does it feel not to fear the afterlife?"

"The abyss is a void. You can't fear something when it's nothing."

He's never told us where his desire to fuck while he's on the brink of dying comes from. But that's what connects the three of us. We've each witnessed something that's fractured our minds and fostered a deviancy so deep under our skin that we'll probably never be able to escape it. But as I stare at the sweet angel unconscious on the bed, I can't wonder if bringing her into our madness is going too far. The root of my existence is a demonic man corrupting a pure woman.

I press the palms of my hands to my eyes, wishing to vanish my lust for her. This is how it starts. This is where I'll break and how the darkness wins. I've never crossed that line until her. I have to save her from us, from me. "We don't need her."

"Maybe not. But we all want her, and that's never happened before. Come on, Dec. She's the first girl you've ever touched. You didn't even think about it. It wasn't hours of you putting yourself through agony just to look at her. She's the key."

"The key to eternal damnation," I mumble under my breath.

"You were raised Catholic. Fucking doom and gloom. You see her as a bad thing, but what if she's your salvation? Look at her."

My eyes fall on her soft face.

"She's the one."

"There's no such thing as 'the one.' The concept of soulmates is a deluded little girl's fantasy."

Lorne laughs. "You're talking to me about fantasies when you believe in a man upstairs?"

I don't answer his question. There's no point. That's the thing most religious people don't understand about atheists. They're as firm in their beliefs as we are in ours. Sometimes you have to remain silent in your words to stay strong in your convictions.

"No words of wisdom from that scripture of yours?"

"There are no words that can crack a heart that's sealed. What would be the point of giving you the gun when all you'll do is point it at me?"

Before Lorne can say anything, his phone rings. "Hello," he answers.

I can't make out who he's talking to, but I'd wager that it's Cas.

"I'll send Declan, and I'll take her home."

Lorne hangs and meets my gaze. "Go meet Cas. Take care of Peter tonight."

My stomach churns. It's the same reaction every time. I know what I'm about to do is wrong, but I do it anyway.

I stare at my hands, focusing on the lines covering my open palms. Minor roads that map the various directions my life could have taken. Knowing I choose the path leading me away from salvation every day. "Christ Jesus came into the world to save sinners—and I am the worst of them all."

Lorne scoffs. "Sometimes you need to do God's work because he's too lazy to clean up the mess he created."

"You don't believe a word you just said."

"No, but you do."

Chapter 12

Caspian

I was two years old the first time I saw a man die. They bludgeoned his head with a hammer because he owed my dad five dollars. That death probably wouldn't have done much damage, but my dad decided to give me a dead man's hand to occupy me so he and his henchmen could work in peace. That fucked up shit makes a lasting impression, especially on a two-year-old. Most dads give their sons a train set or a truck. Not my pop. He gave me a severed hand.

I turn up the collar of my black coat with one hand, the other on the handle of the flimsy motel door. I scan the dark parking lot before jogging to my car—an old black Chevy truck. I only drive it when I'm about to get bloody.

I reach into the cab and smirk as I pull out the black medical bag. I might not kill someone for five dollars, but the apple didn't fall too far from the tree. Dad didn't give me much in life, but he sure passed on the lust for the kill.

I slam the door and stroll back to the room. Peter is tied to the cheap metal bed frame, his eyes bloodshot and wild. He cried like a little bitch. I'm surprised the guy didn't tucker himself out. I thought most babies passed out after they wailed like lunatics.

I open the bag and place the white towel on the scratched-up thrift store desk. I can use a gun and get the job done with no bells and whistles, but where's the fun in that? My father would be terribly disappointed if I didn't take my time and enjoy the art. That's exactly what killing is, a motherfucking art form.

I turn to Peter and laugh at the shock on his face. He's spreadeagled on the bed, his legs tied to the footboard and arms to the headboard.

"I should get one of these bed frames for my room. I'm going to kill you, but it can be multi-purpose. The bed frame you can fuck or blow someone's brains out. Mind you, I'm not so much into blowing brains out. I enjoy taking my time in all extra-curricular activities. Slow and steady for optimum satisfaction. No one likes a wham, bam, thank you, ma'am." I chuckle. "Well, maybe you would right now, but that would make me mediocre, and I'm anything but. You could say I'm a perfectionist."

Peter doesn't say a word. I'm sure he wants to. He'd beg, tell me how he's sorry, he'll never look at my Sunshine again, and move to a deserted island. I always loved hearing those last words, but it got boring after a while. No one has originality. It's all the same thing, over and over again. The mundane is trivial and lackluster.

So now I gag and duct tape the fuckers' mouths and examine their body language instead of torturing my ears with their pathetic pleas.

"Do you know what's beautiful about serial killers? I don't know why I'm asking. I'm just gonna tell you. They fucking make it a show. Not a simple slitting of someone's throat or shooting them in the temple, or poisoning. They make it an extravaganza. I sometimes wonder if Da Vinci had the same buzz when he worked on a piece of art. When he brushed against the canvas to create the Mona Lisa. Do you think it was the same as this?"

A muffled scream erupts as Peter's body jerks when the scalpel blade traces along his thigh.

"Oh, Peter. How fucking rude of me." I rip off the duct tape, and he screams for help. "Please don't waste your breath. The room is soundproof. Why do you think we use this spot? You can scream until you pass the fuck out, but no one will hear you." I rush back to the desk and pull out the mustard, ketchup, mayonnaise, and A1 Sauce. "Which one's your favorite? I want to say you're a ketchup guy. It's a juvenile condiment, and you're a big baby. You couldn't even handle a little flesh wound."

Peter bites his bottom lip as he stares at me. I move closer and stab the scalpel in his leg. "Peter, it's rude not to answer someone when they ask you a question. I know I don't seem like the type who cares much for manners, but I assure you they're very important to me."

I lift my Rubber Soul t-shirt and display the word carved into my abdomen. *Ungrateful.* "My father did this to me when I was seven after I was impolite to one of his lady friends. She tried to touch my cock, but good ol' Dad didn't care. She had something he wanted, and I was the currency. Dad thought I should shut up and let her fuck me. She was the first person I killed. I fucked her with the twelve-inch blade of a hunting knife. Pounded that pedo pussy good and hard until she bled out nice and slow."

"Mayo. I like mayo the best out of those."

I smirk and pull out the Carolina Reaper hot sauce. "Mayo. Another generic sauce. That would have been my second choice." I hold the bottle of hot sauce up to Peter, smirking as I pop the lid. "I like spicy things myself." I tilt the bottle over his leg and watch as one red drop cascades from the bottle and falls directly on the open wound I made a few moments ago.

Screams of pure agony echo through the room.

"Peter, you need to stop that. It's making me hard." Peter's eyes bulge. "Oh, you can relax. I won't fuck you. I've got standards, and human trash doesn't cut it."

"That's rich coming from you," Peter says through tears. "You've got a reputation, Cas. You and Lorne fucking girls while Declan does whatever he does in the corner. You talk about having standards, but the three of you are into some fucked up shit."

"I was waiting, but it seems you're eager to start." I lift the drill out of the bag and rapidly nail his feet to the mattress. His screams are a symphony to my ears, as if Bach himself is in the room with us. "We may be into some fucked up shit, Peter, but the girls we fuck are all willing participants. We don't have to drug them to bang them." I move back to the desk and pull out a paring knife.

"How big is that thing, anyway? Four inches, hard? I grip his cock at the base and hold it on the bed. Peter screams in agony as I slice a tiny piece off the head. "It's three and a half inches now."

Peter's shrill screams permeate my ears. "Maybe I should watch horror movies while I get sucked off cause this shit really does it for me."

I pop the lid of the mayo bottle and let a dollop of the white, creamy substance fall onto the piece of dick. "If you close your eyes and think hard, it will probably taste like a hotdog."

"You're fucking nuts. You're a fucking cannibal."

I turn to him, presenting the fork. "Oh, no, Peter. I like sucking dick, and cum is one of my favorite flavors, but this little morsel is all for you."

"You're a fucking delusional if you think I'm eating that."

I step toward him. "It's cute that you think you have an option."

Peter forms a straight line with his lips, thinking that'll stop me. I pinch his nostrils between my thumb and index finger and squeeze. Time ticks. Peter struggles for breath while I demonstrate my dominance. Breath play isn't for the weak. I've held my best friend's face while he thrashed underneath me, and I've learned a thing or two. I know exactly when someone's going to pass out or die.

"Peter, I don't want you to die right now. I'd be disappointed if my fun was ruined."

He thrashes until his mouth flings open, and I shove in the fork. "Be a good boy and make sure you chew your food properly. I'd hate for you to swallow it whole."

Peter gags with each movement of his jaw, and tears fall from his eyes. He convulses with the natural urge to spit out his cock.

I tut. "You should've picked ketchup."

We turn to the door as it opens. My hand is ready at my gun tucked in the back of my jeans.

"Lorne told me to come here," Declan starts but then his eyes move to Peter. "Jesus Christ, Cas. You have to make a show of this?"

"Taking the lord's name in vain, Dec? That's a sin for you, isn't it? If you want, I can fuck you and beat it away with my belt. I know it's not the most convenient place, but all this torture is making me hard as fuck. Look at all the blood. It's so fucking hot. I think he's bled the most." I point to Peter's bloody and mangled cock. "It's like a never-ending stream."

"I'm not fucking you here, you lunatic."

I pout, jutting out my bottom lip. "Fine. You can watch him eat his supper."

"You're feeding him?"

"What do you think the blood is from? He's having his last supper."

Declan swings the ax by his side as he walks over to Peter.

I jump in front, a barrier between Peter and Declan. "Whoa, whoa. I still have something left to do."

"You cut off a piece of his dick and made him eat it. What other fucked up shit you got up your sleeve?"

I raise my index finger and walk over to the table, lifting the electric drill. Peter's eyes bug out as I move next to him and hold the drill over his face. "Remember what I told you would happen if you ever came near our girl again?"

Peter shakes his head as I pull his right eye open and push the drill in. "Please, no!" Peter screams. "Please!"

"I might be a crazy motherfucker, but I'm true to my word."

Blood spurts from his eye. Once I'm done with the drill, I place it on the bed and dig my fingers into his eye socket, ripping it from the tendons. "Watch with that good eye, Peter."

I bark out a laugh as I drop the eye on my foot and kick up to keep it in play. "Hmm, it's harder to play hacky sack with an eye than I thought."

"God have mercy on your soul, Cas," Declan says as he raises the ax and steps to Peter.

Peter swallows, tears falling down his face as he stares at Declan. "You're as crazy as he is."

"Probably, but unlike him, I have empathy. It's hard being trapped in the materialistic nature of this world. You can't think about what comes next. You can only think about what needs to happen now. There's a plan for us all, Peter, and yours seems to have been to be coerced by the devil."

"What the fuck are you talking about?" Peter screams.

"It's an eye for an eye, Peter. It's the only way to pay for our earthly sins."

With those last words, Declan lifts his ax. Peter's head falls off the bed and rolls to my feet. "You really are a killjoy."

"He's not food, Cas. You can't play with him."

"I'm gonna tear your ass apart cause something is gonna feel good today."

Chapter 13

Noelle

"Fuck," a voice groans. "Who knew jerking off to a sleeping girl would be so damn satisfying?"

I scrunch my eyes closed, shielding them from the sudden flood of light. My head feels muddled and incoherent thoughts form.

Two figures stand before me; one bent over, his hands gripping the quilt draped over the foot of the bed. With blurred eyes, I watch as his body jolts back and forth in fast movements. The other is behind him. I can't make out their faces as they're wearing masks.

All I see are firm hands holding the bent figure by the shoulders.

Sticky liquid falls on my face. I try to open my mouth but fail. My lips are glued together. No, not glued. Tape of some sort. My mouth is sealed shut. I tug at my arms, but they're bound, along with my feet.

Another shadowy figure crosses my vision, arms crossed—a spectator.

The last thing I remember is Peter handing me a drink. I don't usually take drinks from strangers, but since he was so intent on impressing my father, I figured I would be safe. I'm so fucking stupid.

"I'm going to remove the tape, but if you scream, I'll shove my cock down your throat and choke you with it."

My blood runs cold. They're going to rape me. It's not just Peter who's going to violate me. It seems he's invited a group of friends to participate.

His hands are shockingly gentle. He pulls the tape slowly from one corner of my mouth, confusing me with his tenderness. I assumed that any man who wanted to rape me would rip it off, unconcerned about the damage they would leave in their wake.

"My dad can pay you." I sob. "We've got money. You don't need to do this."

The one above clears his throat. "Your dad can't give us what we want."

"What do you want?"

"You."

"I'm not an object."

Warm hands grip my bare thighs. I look down and find that I'm completely naked. My legs are tied up, and my vagina is exposed to the masked man's eyes. All I see is the haunted gray of his irises.

"We know you're not an object," he groans. "You're Madonna and the whore. The sun and the moon. Paradise and Hell. Salvation and damnation. You're the meaning of life."

His words hit me like a fist. They're shocking, deranged, and oddly sweet. I'm confused about how I can find anything sweet in a situation like this, where I'm tied up and my life could very well hang in the balance.

I look at the man above me and freeze. My eyes have finally adjusted, and even though they're all wearing black ski masks, those dark green eyes can't be shrouded. "Lorne?"

Large hands move to the bottom of the mask, lifting it slowly above his head. "Hey, there, pretty Snow."

Snow. He called me that from the moment he first saw me. He's taken my last name and added his twist. I assumed he was mocking me, but I know that's not the case when he looks at me like he's beholding something majestic.

"What are you doing, Lorne?" I look at the two figures at the foot of the bed. "I'm guessing you're Cas and Declan."

"At your service, Sunshine," the man groans as he holds the other's head aggressively on the bed. "Fuck, if looking at your cunt makes me come like this, I'm curious to see what fucking it will do."

I'm confused. I'm tied up and wet. So wet that I think I could come from just his words. I turn to Lorne, and he smirks. The little shit knows I'm wet.

"What do you want, Snow?"

"I want you to let me go."

His finger moves along the cum on my face, trailing it over my skin like a child moving finger paint on paper. He carries it to my lips and glides the cum along them. "You don't want that, Snow. No, you want us to fuck you like animals. You want to know what it's like to be railed so hard that you can't walk straight."

My tongue darts out, and I get a small taste of his salty-sweet flavor. My eyes close of their own accord as my mind wages war with itself. This isn't me. I'm the good girl. The sweet girl. I'm the girl who does everything she's supposed to. "You shall not eat it, nor shall you touch it, lest you die."

"What did you say?" Declan asks.

"I'm contemplating the dangers of giving in to men like you."

Declan shoves Cas onto the bed and leaves the room without a word, slamming the door behind him.

Sadness tugs at my heart over his reaction. "Did I say something wrong?"

"No, he's fucked up. We're all fucked up." Lorne turns to Cas and nods.

"I can't believe I have to deal with him while you get to stare at her," Cas grumbles.

He says something under his breath, but I can't make it out. I can only focus on his massive erection as he stalks to the door after Declan.

A warm breath along my ear. "It's impressive, isn't it?"

"What is?" I feign ignorance because that man's penis is like a damn elephant in a China shop. He gives a new meaning to the word anaconda.

Lorne raises an eyebrow, "Snow, you can cut the act. You're practically drooling."

My eyes catch his. "You're no slouch, but Jesus, that's a horse's cock."

A warm, boisterous chuckle fills the room. "Don't I know it." He's silent for a moment, then adds in a soft, deductive tone, "He knows how to use it too. I promise it'll be worth your while."

Briar's voice crashes into my mind. "Fuck them. Fuck, if you don't want to do it, call me, and I'll ride them until they call uncle."

I thrash my bound arms, irrationally angry at the idea of her going anywhere near them. But also, I hate that I don't have Briar's confidence. If she were here, she'd bend herself up like a pretzel and have the time of her life.

For Briar, sex is easy and fun. It's no strings attached. For me, sex is traumatic. I wasn't sure I wanted it that first time. My vagina sure wasn't wet. Jimmy didn't seem to care about checking in on me, either. He shoved it in, and after two pumps, he rolled over and asked me if I came as hard as him. The experience was so horrible that I'd rather use my wand than look at a man.

"Where'd you go?"

Lorne's deep voice pulls me from my thoughts. "To the past."

Lorne shakes his head, his hair flopping over his emerald eyes. "The past is never a good place. You try to outrun it, but it always seems to be there, lingering."

"For a psycho, you're profound."

He sits beside me, pulling a cigarette out of the pack and lighting it. "Profound isn't always a good thing. Usually, it means you've lived too much of life."

"What are you going to do to me if I say no? If I don't want to be a part of your merry little band."

"Let you go."

"That's it? I say no, and you let me go on my merry way to live peacefully, far from your prying eyes?"

Lorne takes a drag of his cigarette, a lopsided smirk on his full, kissable lips. "I never said we'd let you live peacefully." He turns to me, wiping the cum off my face with a clean cloth. "You're kerosene, Snow, and we're the flames. Once the two have been introduced, there's no going back. The explosion has to happen.

But as fucked up as we are, we could never harm you." He takes another hit of the cigarette, inhaling deeply. "Besides, you help him, and no one has ever been able to help him."

"Help who?"

"Declan."

"Declan? The guy who stormed out of here like I killed his mother?"

"The same. He's got issues. You triggered him, but trust me, Snow; you're the key."

I stare up at the ceiling. "Is that a noose up there?"

Lorne peers up and laughs. "Never said Declan was the only one with issues."

I take in the thick brown rope hanging from the ceiling. What kind of fucked up shit are these three into? I should run, tell them to fuck off, and move to a different continent. But Lorne's lost expression and sad smile make me say something I fear I may regret in the worst way. "Okay."

"Okay?"

"Yes. Untie my arms and legs and get the other two nutjobs back in here. If I'm going to do this, we need ground rules."

Chapter 14

Noelle

I look out the window at the surrounding forest. Trees as far as the eye can see. Someone could easily get lost out there with no way home. It's a refuge for the lonely and a shroud for those who wish to hide...

Cas walks into the room first. His almost-black hair is wet. He plops himself on the bed beside me with a goofy smile like a child on Christmas morning. "You couldn't resist my cock, huh?"

I turn to Lorne. He holds his hands in the air, feigning innocence with a smirk. "He was listening at the door."

Cas gives me a sly wink. "I'll go easy on you the first time."

Declan is the last to enter the room, his hands working what appears to be a rosary set. I only know because my grandmother constantly fidgeted with one.

He refuses to look at me, and I hate it. "Can you come here, please, Declan?"

His head shoots up, and he hesitates for a moment before he steps forward. Declan reminds me of a stray beaten so badly he's not sure if he should run or bite you. He sits on the other side of the bed and stares out the window.

"I'll only try this if you're in."

He lifts his head, and his mesmerizing steel-gray eyes glare at me. "For God knows that on the day you eat of it, your eyes will be opened, and you will be like God, knowing good and evil."

I'm taken aback by his quoting scripture.

"Genesis 3:5. Though, I'm not sure if I'm the apple or the serpent," I say with an amused smile.

His eyes bore into mine, and the silence in the room thickens as we all await his response. "You're Eve."

"So I guess I'm about to take a bite of the apple, and my entire world is going to change?"

"You took that bite the first time I saw you. And as much as this is wrong, and I know I'll pay for the choices I'll make because of you, I can't walk away. I've searched for peace my entire life and never found it." Declan stares out the window, swallowing hard as if fighting an internal battle. "Until you."

If this were a scene in a movie, the girl would leap out of bed and jump into the man's arms. The credits would roll, and the audience would leave on a euphoric high of love.

But this isn't a movie. You wouldn't find these guys in a rom-com. Something tells me they're messy, with truckloads of baggage that I'm probably not equipped to deal with. But my gut tells me to jump in feet first without a second thought.

I scoot closer to Declan and place my hands on his face. The rosary clatters to the hardwood floor.

His panicked eyes shoot to mine. "What are you doing?"

"I'm going to kiss you."

He jumps off the bed as if I've lit him on fire. "I can't."

I pull back as if he's slapped me in the face. My insecurities churn, and I want the ground to open up and swallow me whole. The way Lorne was talking, I assumed they all wanted me, but Declan's reaction made it seem like I repelled him.

"Before we start, you gotta know a few things," Cas says as he rubs the back of his neck.

"I'm not going to be one of your flings."

Cas tilts his head and smirks. "You're far from a fling, Sunshine."

"Not according to Declan."

Cas laughs. "Because he won't kiss you? I've been fucking him for years, and he still hasn't kissed me, but I tell you what." He points to Declan. "He'd take a bullet for me and not think twice. We've all got baggage, and that shit left a mark. His story isn't mine to tell, but if you stay, if you stick with us, you'll be the queen, and we'll be your army."

Again, I'm taken aback at how sweet and deranged these guys are. "I don't want to be one of those girls you all fuck and then discard."

Cas smirks. “Sunshine, from the moment we saw you, we seem to have forgotten other girls exist. But maybe we should talk about what we’re capable of.”

Short of wanting to chop me up and throw me in the forest, I’m confident I can handle it. I know who these guys are. Lorne works with my dad, and the men who work with him aren’t necessarily good people. The Syndicate is a group of dangerous men who aren't afraid of crossing lines. “What is it?”

“We like certain things.”

“What kind of things?”

Cas digs inside the front pocket of his jeans and flips a switchblade. I don’t even process what’s happening until a crimson line forms on my skin. “That was nothing. I will hurt you. I like blood.”

“Blood, how? Like a vampire? Do you drink it?”

He nods. “Yes, and I also like to cut. The sight of it gets me going.” He gazes at Lorne and clears his throat. “You know what we do, right?”

“Yes, you work with my dad. I love my father, but I’m not stupid. I know what he’s involved in.”

“I’ve been known to fuck one of these two in the blood of someone I’ve killed.”

I'm completely turned on. Am I a sick person? Guess it makes sense why some people want sex while watching a horror movie. The same part of the brain gets switched on. "Um, you're not going to kill me, are you?"

He laughs and winks at me. "Haven't killed anyone during sex yet. But sex with me hurts. Sex with all of us does. We like it rough, fast, and dangerous."

"Will you stop if I ask you to?"

"Absolutely. You'll have a safe word and gestures when you can't speak."

"Why wouldn't I be able to speak?"

Chapter 15

Lorne

Insecurity is something I've never experienced until this moment. I'm not worried about sex. I always knock that out of the park, but I saw how she stared at the noose. It's not a simple thing to explain to people, and I sure as fuck don't want her to run before we even get started. But if we want something more than one night, we have to come clean.

"You noticed the noose earlier?"

She looks up, "Yes. I thought it was some sort of emo decor." She points to Cas's Joy Division T-shirt.

"Maybe you're one of those weird Ian Curtis fans. The kind who takes everything a little too far?"

"It's more like an INXS fan who shares a kink with Michael Hutchence."

She cocks her head. "Micheal died by—" Her eyes go wide when it clicks. "Oh."

Some people like a faint pressure on their necks while they fuck. I want to be on the brink of death as I come. "That's not all."

Her eyebrows furrow together. "I'm not sure how much crazier this can get."

I wouldn't blame her if she ran out of here like she was on fire. I wouldn't allow her to get very far, but I would understand her motives.

"Show me."

I flinched as if she hit me. "You can't handle it."

"My parents were together for over twenty years when my mom died. My dad didn't hide any part of himself from my mom. She didn't always agree with his choices, but she loved my father, his dark, broken pieces and all. Not showing me your full truth means you're not ready to handle me."

"You sure he never stepped out on her?" Cas snickers.

I glare at him, and he shuts up. I love the guy, but he needs a fucking muzzle sometimes.

Noelle turns to Cas, biting her bottom lip, and tilts her head. "Is that what you would do to me, Cas? Step out on me? Because I'll tell you one thing. I will never fucking tolerate cheating. I know I might not look like the typical girl you see in magazines, but I'm a fucking catch. I have boatloads of self-respect."

"What the fuck is that supposed to mean?" I snap. "You're fucking better than any girl in a magazine. No one can hold a candle to you."

Her words are self-assured and confident, but her sad eyes are like a punch to my gut. I want to pummel Cas and beat his dense head in. The little fucker.

I brush my finger along her jawline. "None of us will ever cheat on you. If one of us thinks about it, the other two will kill him."

Cas jumps in front of her with his hands in the air. "Sunshine, no one has to kill me if I ever look at another woman. I'll chop my dick off first."

She laughs, and it's like a chorus of angels. "Guess you're the one who doesn't like to be outdone, huh?"

"When you have the hottest girl you've ever seen in front of you, the only girl who's makes all three of you fuckin' insane in a good way, you're gonna do whatever it takes to make sure she's happy. I know I act like an idiot sometimes, but trust me, Sunshine, I'm anything but." He grabs her hand and slams it against his dick. "You feel that?"

Noelle licks her lips and nods.

"All I can think about is sinking into your holes and fucking you senseless. It's taking a lot of self-control on my part not to eat you out while you're talking to them. I can smell how turned on you are, and that pretty cunt is bare and begging for my tongue." Cas rips the sheet off her, exposing her naked flesh. The three of us are a pack of wolves with our tongues hanging out and tails wagging. "Actually, spread 'em."

"What?" Noelle asks. Her voice is shaky, but her legs part slowly at Cas's demand.

He doesn't respond. His large hands grip her knees and pull her legs as far apart as he can. "I've been dying for a damn taste."

Her head falls back, and she moans. "You got anything to add to the conversation, Declan?"

Declan rises from the bed and pulls his cock out of the waistband of his jogging pants. He grips his thick erection and works it with his palm as he stares at

Cas's tongue devouring her cunt. "All I can think about is sucking on your clit again. But I also want to hear you choke on my cock."

"Oh, God."

A slap to her tit by Declan's hand. "Dirty girl, using the lord's name like that." He moves his cock to her face and taps her cheek. "Open up."

Declan pushes his cock into her mouth and straddles her neck. I'm careful to watch him because as much as I hope he won't take it too far, I know this act pains him. To Declan, it's not fucking. To him, it's a step towards damnation; with the way his fucked up brain works, he might kill her to rid himself of evil.

His thumbs are by her eyes, pushing down at her temples. He looks deranged, lost in the black-and-white hellscape of his own creation. "Just like Jesus, I seem to like pretty little whores."

"Declan, turn around. Let her choke on your cock while you eat her out."

He doesn't listen to me. He just keeps pushing his ass toward her mouth. Her gagging fills the room, and my cock surges like never before. I quickly take off my belt and rear it over my head, slashing it along Declan's back.

He moves back, and I hear her gasps for breath. He hisses as his back arches when I hit him again. "Turn around, Declan."

He lifts a knee, then the other, and turns himself around, his ass now behind the crown of her head. The base of his cock is visible, while most of his length is back in her mouth. To my surprise, her hands are on his thighs, and she isn't pushing him away but pulling him closer as if she's desperate to get more of him into her mouth.

Declan falls forward, his tongue out like a cat desperate for water.

"Suck her clit, Dec. She's so fucking sweet," Cas murmurs as his tongue darts in and out of her hole.

I drop the belt and grip the back of Declan's head to hold him in place as I bend to join them. One lick of her pussy, and I'm a goner. She's a drug I'll crave for the rest of my life. I'll gladly die of an overdose so long as it's from savoring her. Her flavor is distinct, hypnotic, and addictive.

Cas glides one finger in her pussy as his tongue meets mine and Declan's by her clit. I move my hand and join his finger with one of mine. We move back and forth, and her hips buck against us. Declan moans, and it vibrates along her pussy. He, too, pushes a finger into her cunt, and we work her pussy in unison until her legs stiffen.

"I want you to drench us, Sunshine," Cas growls as his finger moves along mine and curls to hit her G-spot. "I want to drink until I'm full."

She screams as all three of us apply pressure. She bucks beneath us to be free, but that isn't going to happen. And then the first sprays of her cum splash us in the face.

I grip Declan's hair and bring him down to her cunt, watching as her pussy drenches his face. "This is divine. It's the only holy water you should concern yourself with."

Chapter 16

Declan

My entire being wants this girl. No, *needs* her. Like I need my next breath. Every ounce of restraint I've held onto crumbles to dust. I drink her into me like I'm taking the sacrament of Christ, discovering the Holy Grail within her folds. With each lash of my tongue on her clit, I draw one step closer to God.

Her voice. I can never escape that voice.

These are lies, Declan. It's the devil's work tryi[illegible] deceive you. You're a sinful boy with sinful urges. G[illegible] out your demons. Beat them to ensure they leave you be. She's tempting you. They all tempt you.

I jump off the bed and scamper to the corner of the room. Cas and Lorne don't notice that my tongue is no longer entwined with theirs. Before me is a vision of Sodom and Gomorrah, naked bodies, and depravity. My cock aches with the need for release. It unleashes the burden she's caused in our lives. The beast within me wants to ravish her, to fuck her until she passes out, to rip her apart. I want to ruin her and use her body until I've had my fill.

"Now the works of the flesh are evident: sexual immorality, impurity, sensuality, idolatry, sorcery, enmity, strife, jealousy, fits of anger, rivalries, dissensions, divisions, envy, drunkenness, orgies, and things like these. I warn you, as I warned you before, that those who do such things will not inherit the kingdom of God."

Cas's head shoots up, and he glares at me. "Not this shit again."

My eyes form into slits as I glare at him. It's so easy for him to live in the moment, to fuel his body on pure lust. Cas is the human embodiment of the deadly sins. He doesn't treat his body as a temple, a sacred vessel that belongs to God. Cas's life is one huge indulgence.

He stands, and his large frame seems bigger than life. His steps are an earthquake about to pull me under. "Fuck that bitch. Fuck every fucking thing her cunt ass said to you."

I turn away, but he grips my chin and moves my head back, forcing me to look into his eyes. "I didn't drill holes in her eyes so she could live rent-free in your head."

Flashes of her mangled body appear in my mind. The mixed emotions I felt that day still fester in my heart. By killing her, Cas and Lorne freed me from her shackles, but a part of me also felt sorrow because she was the only mother I ever knew. "She was trying to save me. To show me the path to God."

Cas's arm is on my throat. He doesn't blink as he slams my body against the wall with one large arm, holding me still. I flinch as his other hand viciously grips my cock. "That cunt showed you shit. She took a traumatized little boy who was found sitting in shit and vomit after his whore mother and drug dealer father decided they loved heroin more than their kid, and instead of helping you heal, she beat you."

"We are all born of sin. She was trying to cure me of the evil I came from."

Cas flips me so my stomach is against the wall and my back is to his chest. His finger moves up and down my ass crack. "Give me a fuckin' break. You were a kid. Kids don't know good and evil. They're taught that shit by the fucking assholes who raise them. Your mother was strung out, and your dad was a low-life piece of shit. But your aunt, that cunt was the worst of them all. I regret not making her suffer more. I should have fucked her cunt with the drill and cut her nipples off while doing it."

Rage festers in me. I grip his arm and push him back before facing him.

"That's it, Dec. Let it out. You want to fight? We can fight. You want to fuck? I'll fuck you until you can't see straight. I'll even nail your hands to your fucking cross while I do it. But you are gonna fuck her, and you're going to make her realize how fucking angelic she is. You can be a complete cocksucker to Lorne and me, but that fucked up religious shit in your head doesn't touch her."

I don't say a word because no matter what I do and say to Cas, it won't make an impact. I've hurt him in so many ways, and he's still here. The guy might be a complete psycho, but he's loyal. Still, I want him to hurt. I want him to be angry and mental. I want him reeling, just like me.

I walk past him to Noelle. Her eyes are on the two of us like she's watching a horror movie. I hate what I'm about to do, but I'm doing it, anyway.

I clasp her heels and pull her legs apart, pushing them toward her chest. Without warning or tenderness, I ram my cock in her pussy and listen to her scream.

Chapter 17

Noelle

He's an anaconda or a shapeshifting horse.

I didn't know it was humanly possible for a penis to be this big. And here I am, staring at three men blessed by the gods. I'm grateful I'm so wet because if I wasn't, that thing he calls a penis would be ripping me apart.

He slaps my breasts, and I want more. He isn't gentle. Whatever this is, it's not just about desire.

I turn away, focusing on the tree branches outside the window, but he grips my face firmly and pulls my eyes to him. "Be a good slut, Eve. Look at me and only me when I'm balls deep in you. I want you to know who's tearing this tight little pussy apart."

I'm confused because I'm scared *and* aroused. His gaze is full of hate, desire, and vengeance. It's almost like Declan is fucking me, hoping to outrun something.

"Open your mouth."

My instinct is to obey him, not to poke the bear when he's already feral, but I also want to push him. These men aren't gentle. Their entire world is violence and pain. If I'm going to be with them, I need a clear grasp of what they're capable of.

"Fuck you, Declan."

He grips my hair at the base of my crown and tugs. The pain is excruciating, but that's not what stuns me. It's the fact that I enjoy it. I clench around him, and at that moment, he does something I've never seen him do. He smiles. "My pretty little slut likes pain as much as I do."

His open palm presses against the side of my head, pushing my face into the pillow. His other hand gropes my breast with such force that I'm fearful he'll rip it off. The tip of his thumb invades the side of my mouth. "When I tell you to do something, my little whore, you do it."

He pulls at the side of my mouth until, from sheer pain, my lips part, and he takes that moment to place four fingers into my mouth. I gag from his invasion, and he laughs, pulling his wet fingers out, along with trails of saliva, that he wipes his hand on my face. "There, now you're a proper whore. Better get used to it, Eve. It's what you deserve for being a fucking Jezebel."

His actions should repulse me, but all I can think about is how to get more. I've lived a certain way my entire life, always the good girl, doing the right things, knowing when to talk and when to stay silent. The apple of my father's eye, always trying to make him proud. It's exhausting living for others, bending for them. But with Declan, I feel free. I like that he doesn't see me as perfect but wants me, anyway. He isn't fixated on the shine. He craves the darkness.

"Is that all you got?" I yell in his face.

He stills. I'm not sure what he's going to do, but the anticipation is exciting. This sense of danger is like opium throbbing in my veins, and I seem to have a newfound thirst for it.

"Careful there, Snow. He's not all there," Lorne says softly but firmly.

"None of us are all there. Cas is the Bellview Butcher. Killed his first man at nine. You're the head of the

Miller family, one of the most notorious mob families in the United States. You're known for your unforgiving wrath."

I grip Declan's face, looking deep into his eyes. "And you're known as the Last Rite. The killer who allows his victims to seek retribution before he decapitates them."

I turn to them all, frustration brewing in me. "My entire life, I've been the chubby sweet girl. The unseen girl. Girls like me, invisible girls who are never wanted, who don't appeal to guys who look like you. see everything." Anger rolls off my body in waves. "I know I'm not the hot girl who walks in the room and draws attention. I'm not what the world sees as desirable, but I'm not an idiot, so don't treat me like one."

An animalistic growl takes over the room. Strong arms wrap around me and I'm lifted as if I weigh nothing.

The harsh lights of the bathroom flash on. I gaze at myself in the large mirror. Lorne's chin is resting on my head. He doesn't appear sinister right now. He looks thoughtful and sweet. Two words I doubt anyone would use to describe him.

"Look in the mirror."

My reflection greets me.

"Mirror, mirror on the wall, Noelle Snow is the fairest of them all." His finger glides on my cheek. "This is the face that could launch a thousand ships. You're the kind of beauty men wage wars for. The kind of perfection that can destroy empires." I jerk as his hands fist my breasts. "From the moment I saw you, all I've been able to think about is sliding my cock between these big, sexy tits and coming on your pretty face."

Romantic and depraved. Those are the two words I would use to describe Lorne Miller. He's talking about my face, but as I stare in the mirror, I focus on my thick thighs and stomach rolls.

"And this," he says as his hands grip my stomach, "I'm going to hold on to as I pound your sweet cunt into oblivion. Every inch of you is sexy. Every part makes my cock hard as steel. You're perfect, Snow. You're the only girl all three of us have ever craved. The one made for us. We aren't perfect, but we're perfect for you."

"I don't want you to hurt me," I whisper, admitting the truth. "I'm used to people using me."

"We'll always protect your heart, but we will hurt your body." His hand moves off my breasts and he slams my head against the mirror as he kicks my legs apart. He shoves his dick in my pussy with one hard thrust. "It's who we are, Snow. It's the only way we know how to love; through pain, blood, and violence."

He yanks my head back by my hair and grabs my throat, his fingers pushing down aggressively on the sides. His lips move to the shell of my ear, grazing my earlobes. "You want to see who we are, Snow? You want to dive into the darkest depths of hell?"

"Yes," I pant.

"I'm warning you, pretty Snow. Once we show you our truth, you'll become our prisoner. We'll never let you go."

My mind screams at me to run, to get out while I can. But my body melts under his forceful touch. "I need to know the truth."

Lorne pulls me from the bathroom by my throat. I open my mouth to grasp air, but all I do is wheeze. His grip is so tight that panic rises within me. He throws me on the bed.

Chapter 18

Lorne

"I wasn't planning on throwing you in the deep end, but some people can't dip their toes before diving."

Her breaths are shallow as her chest rises and falls beneath me. She digs her nails into my biceps as she tries to anchor herself. I wonder if that's how we appear to her, an ocean she's desperate not to drown in, so she has no option but to tread water.

Her eyes search mine as her body trembles, from fear or excitement, I'm not sure. "What are you going to do to me?"

"I'm going to force you to watch."

I jump on the bed and grab the brown noose hanging from the ceiling. "This is me, Snow. Showing you something that only two other people know. Two people who would take a bullet for me. I'm trusting you, Snow, because you matter."

Without saying a word, Cas is behind me, one arm wrapped around my waist and a bottle of lube in his hand. "Join in anytime, Sunshine."

He grips my cock, spreading my pre-cum on the head of my dick with his thumb. "Make yourself useful, Declan. Get on your knees and open your mouth."

Declan grips the rosary in his hand, the attached cross falling into view. He crawls onto the bed, one knee then the other until he's facing my cock. He moves his hand and replaces Cas and does something that makes my dick twitch. With the rosary in his hand, he wraps it around my shaft and slides it up from the tip of my cock to the base. There's a perverse pleasure from having him use something he finds so divine in an act he views as sinful.

"Our Father, who art in heaven, hallowed be thy name. Thy kingdom come, thy will be done, on earth, as it is in heaven. Give us this day our daily bread and forgive us our trespasses as we forgive those who trespass against us. And lead us not into temptation, but deliver us from evil."

I sigh, frustrated. "Stop preaching and start sucking."

"I've become a servant to demons and lost my way from the heavenly father. I've cast out his light in favor of this."

"God and I are very similar, Declan. But when I fuck you, it feels good. My rod doesn't make you scream in agony. It makes you moan in bliss."

Declan opens his mouth. I grip the back of his head and propel my hips forward, impaling the back of his throat with sheer force. "Does this remind you of church, Declan? On your knees, but instead of begging for answers from your imaginary daddy, it's for my cock."

My dress shirt pools at my feet, unraveling the road maps of my life I wear on my skin. Cold liquid glides down my ass as Cas holds his blade to my side.

I hear Noelle's audible hiss. My eyes lock with hers, and behind the rich brown of her irises, I see a sadness. She offers me a small smile as a tear glides down her soft cheek. My little Snow, always wanting to help animals, even a monstrous beast like me.

I realize what my flesh looks like, a mangled mess of cuts I've tried and failed to cover with intricate tattoos.

"We've all got scars, Snow. Some of us wear them on our skin, while others carry them on the inside. They are what forge us into who we are. You don't need to be sad for mine because, as vicious as they may seem, they've led me to this point and to you."

We don't have to say a word because, in the silence, there is an understanding. That's the moment I know she will always belong to us, whether or not she's with us. Because of her pure heart and empathetic nature, she doesn't regard us as disgusting animals. She's the only one who can move past it all and see us as men. I hope it's as men worthy of her love.

Chapter 19

Caspian

This happens when you're driven by your [illegible] fuckin' cock. I understand how horrific we must appear. I'm not dumb or blind. My eyes are on Sunshine. She's crying, which makes me want to beat Lorne's head in. It's fucked up that her tears are making me hard, but I'm concerned for her, and it's not because I assume she'll run.

What's crazy is that I've never been worried about a chick before. I don't even go down on them. My mentality is to fuck 'em. Their orgasm isn't my problem. But with her, all I can think about is making her cum so damn much that she'll pass out from it. I want to fall asleep with her cradled in my arms and my cock buried in her pussy or ass. I'm good with either hole.

I lean in and whisper in Lorne's ear, "I should fuck you without lube, so you'll know how fucked up this is."

Lorne doesn't say shit to me. He just lifts his hand and tightens the noose. I should let the fucker strangle himself to death. Instead, I lube my dick and line it up with his asshole as I stab his side with the knife and thrust into his ass.

If this is her reaction to Lorne's flesh, how she'll take it when she sees the horror of my skin? There's a reason I like knives. It's a fucked up reason, and I don't want to think about it, but I know Sunshine will ask, and eventually, I'll have to 'fess up.

With my eyes locked on her, I glide the knife down Lorne's side, cutting a little deeper than I usually would. I groan at the sight of the red fluid oozing from his skin and my mouth waters at the notion of the metallic flavor on my tongue.

My hand tightens around Lorne's stomach as I pull the noose with my free hand. The first time I did this,

I forgot to support his body and almost snapped his neck. "The big, bad, Lorne Miller, nothing but a pathetic fuck boy. How does it feel to have no power and be at my mercy?"

Lorne groans as his body flails, arms and legs shaking like a damn airman. It's fucked up what he makes us do, but I don't judge. His shit is no crazier than my dick getting hard at the sight of blood.

I gaze down at Declan's hand moving the rosary on his dick while his mouth works in a fevered frenzy.

"Cut him down!" Sunshine screams, her palms over her eyes, her body shaking.

I stab the tip of the blade into Lorne again. "This is who we are, beautiful. This is what we do. You wanted the curtains drawn back. Here it is."

Her tears and trembling body make my cock throb. I like it. I enjoy seeing her miserable, but that isn't what's shocking. What rocks me is feeling her emotional pain with my arousal. Remorse hits me. I'm so fucked up that I want to see more of it. That's never happened before.

"He's going to die." She falls to her knees with her hands clasped together as if she's praying. Too bad Declan's back is to her. He'd probably jizz from just the sight. "I'm begging you, please untie him."

"He won't die, but a part of me wants to kill him just to see you beg some more."

She crawls to the foot of the bed. "Declan, please. He's going to die."

Chapter 20

Declan

I grip Lorne's ass as my mouth moves further down his dick. I gag, and bile rises from my throat. This is how I like it. I want his cock to pierce me, to make thinking hard, to be lost in the turmoil and bliss that sinning provides. These are the moments when there's no guilt. No pain.

There's a tug at the hem of my shirt. "Please, Declan, please!"

Her voice is the bright glare of truth shining on our depravity and sickness. I close my eyes and focus on

Lorne's cock twitching in my mouth as my head bops down, desperate for more.

When I'm on my knees being debased, I don't hate myself because it seems like retribution. It makes little sense because everything I do goes against the word of God, but it feels right. But her voice reminds me that I'm a sinner and want to punish her.

I grip her throat with the hand holding the rosary, slamming her onto the bed. My burning gaze is on her as I press the beads forcefully into her delicate flesh. Her fingers grip my hands as her nails puncture my skin, drawing blood. I want to bury myself in her, to debase and control her. The whore is what I want. The Jezebel. At this moment, I don't want to see her purity. I want to see her indecency.

A drop of blood from Lorne's flesh drips onto her forehead. How apropos. I raise my head, staring at Lorne as a disciple would gaze upon Jesus crucified on the cross, my cock raging with need at the sight before me.

Trails of blood glide down Lorne's sides as he shakes. His body lowers as Cas loosens the noose, and he grips the back of my head, holding me firmly to him as he cums in my mouth.

Cas pulls out of Lorne and drops of cum fall onto the bedspread. "Fuck. Why is cum dripping out of an asshole so damn hot? You know, Sunshine, it's pretty fuckin' hot to fill you up like a twinkie." His jaw ticks as his eyes land on my hand against her throat. He jumps off the bed and presses the knife to my throat. "Get your fuckin' hands off her, you goddamn nut job."

I ignore him as cum floods my mouth, and I gaze at Eve. Her face is red, her eyes rolling back. My cock is at full mast, harder than it's ever been. Lorne pulls out of me, but he's too weak from lack of oxygen to do much of anything.

The sting of the knife plummets to my side. "Get your fuckin' hands off her, Declan.

My eyes snap to Cas before I turn to Eve and spit cum directly into her face and watch as it sticks to her eyelashes. I stumble back, and Noelle grabs her throat, wheezy, tears bursting from her eyes, mingling on her face with cum. The imprint of my rosary is vivid on her flesh.

I've mastered keeping my face emotionless, a skill that's come in handy in my life, but at this moment, as I gaze at her, I want to drop to my knees and beg for her forgiveness. But I won't do that because if I show her vulnerability, she'll become the center, and I'll lose faith in everything but her.

"I showed her who I am. That's what I did."

"By trying to strangle her," Cas asks.

He's angry. He actually gives a fuck. Usually, everything is a joke with him. Caspian thinks it's all shits and giggles. When he gets pissed, it means he cares. This is when he's the most vulnerable and the most dangerous. "You could have fucking killed her."

I turn to Noelle. She's on the bed, and Lorne's hand is on hers, but his eyes are slits and focused on me. "Go to your room, Declan, and get ready."

Chapter 21

Noelle

The door slams as Declan walks out of the room. My throat still hurts, but Lorne seems to be a little better. He's sitting up, his feet on the floor. At least I am not scared of him dying anymore.

I take his bloody form, and I don't know what to make of what I witnessed. These men horrify and intrigue me because what I believe to know about them isn't the entire truth.

I've known about Lorne most of my life. First his father, a ruthless rival to mine. After his father's murder, Lorne, the only child, took over the business.

It wasn't because he was qualified; I heard my father say to my mom, it was because of his name. But over the years, Lorne has made a name for himself that rivals his father, so I assumed he just was as horrific. Yet, as I gaze at his back, regarding how it rises and falls in rapid succession, I'm not sure if rumors of his brutality weren't exaggerated.

Cas grips my chin and lifts my head. He's gentle as he examines my neck. It's hard to believe a man who stabbed someone as he came has the same fingers brushing like feathers along my skin. "There seems to be no permanent damage. But that fucker needs to slow his roll. He could've hurt her. This is twice now. I realize he's got some fuckin' issues, but we all do."

Lorne nods and gets up, walking to the bathroom, his broad, sculpted back riddled with blade marks and burn scars. Dear Lord, why does he have so many burn scars? "Take her with you."

"Lorne, you can't be fuckin' serious. She'll run."

Lorne braces his body on the doorframe, one hand on each side. "We are who we are. We can't lie to her and expect her to stay."

Anger flares in me. These men seem to think they can pluck me out of my existence, and I'll do anything they want. "I'm not staying past a week, regardless."

Lorne turns to me, his green eyes ablaze. "What do you mean?"

"I'm surprised you don't know. It seems you notice a little too much about me. At first, I assumed it was because of your connections to my dad, but now I'm not too sure." I shut my mouth, afraid I've given away too much information. My dad always told me that with guys like him, wise guys and criminals, it's better not to offer information because something inconsequential is ammunition to men like him. But my anger is so raw that it shuts down my logical brain. "I got a scholarship to study in France. I leave in a week."

I don't even know why I'm angry. It's not like it matters what these three do. It's not like I won't have a whole life in Paris in a week. My reactions to them and this situation aren't rational, but nothing about these three men is.

There are quick movements on the mattress as Cas jumps up and frantically paces the room. The sharp end of the blade scrapes on his open palm. He's intentionally cutting himself. Cas a cutter?

I take him in as his brow furrows and his shoulders tense. A slice of the knife, and his whole body relaxes. That lasts a few moments at most before he stiffens again. The faint lines of his tattoos make sense, these little dents out of place with the artwork.

"Cas, you're cutting yourself. Your hand is covered in blood."

He glares at me. "It calms me. I either have to do it to you or me. Which would you rather?"

I pause at his question. *Which would you rather?* I rise off the bed and walk to him, placing my hand on his palm as he brings the blade down. It pierces my skin and tears into my flesh. It hurts, but I will not show him that. I want him to pause, to snap out of whatever dark place he's in that makes him need a coping mechanism like this.

Cas' eyes meet mine. "Guess that answers the question."

"I'd much rather you didn't do it to yourself or me, but I don't enjoy seeing any living thing harmed. It hurts me."

"Fuck this shit. I'm going to take care of Declan."

Cas storms out of the room, leaving me reeling and alone with Lorne.

Lorne clears his throat, drawing my attention away from Cas and back to him. "Edward didn't mention that during dinner last month."

"Why would he? Don't you all talk about whatever criminal things you do? Why would he give you the four-one-one on his twenty-two-year-old daughter's education plans?" My eyes take in the bedroom door. "Shouldn't you go after him?"

Lorne chuckles and rubs the back of his neck. "Nah, He'll take whatever it is out on Declan, and they'll both come out winning. Now, back to this trip."

"I received an opportunity to study in Paris, and I'm taking it. It's for six months with the option to extend for a year."

"Guess you'll have to be back for the wedding?"

I glare at him, confused. "What wedding? I'm not even sure if I want to fuck you all yet. Well, I guess I fucked one of you. But you see what I mean. I think marriage is a little premature."

Lorne wheezes as he laughs. "Not us. Your dad and my mother. A fucking marriage of convenience. A merger that will give us all the power in the syndicate. That's why I originally began watching you. I wanted to understand what kind of competition you'd be for a seat at the table. But I soon realized you were as much a threat as a fucking bug I could crush under my feet."

His words are like a slap in the face. My blood chills and my hands shake. Lorne is just like Peter. "You're all the same. A bunch of users."

Lorne approaches me. I retreat until my back hits the wall and I have no more room to distance myself from him.

He glides his nose along my neck before his hot breath meets my ear. "That's how it started. I didn't say that's how it ended. You're so fucking good, Noelle. So fucking good. In a world like mine, purity is non-existent, but there you were, pure as the driven snow. I stopped viewing you as an acquisition and began to see you as a partner. The ying to our yang. The light to our darkness. The virtue to our sin. When I saw how Declan reacted to you, I realized you were the one."

"React to me? He tried to strangle me to death."

Lorne smirks. "Only because he wants you more than he wants God."

"People don't want God, Lorne. God isn't an object. People need him."

Lorne's fingers brush against my sore neck. "All right, I'll play the word manipulation game. Declan needs you more than he needs God."

An ear-shattering scream permeates the room. "What's that?"

"Declan."

"Aren't you going to help him?" I yell. "He sounds like he's in pain."

"He is. He likes it."

I place the palms of my hand on his chest and push with all my strength. "What the fuck is wrong with you?"

He steps back and shrugs. "Everything and nothing."

I open the door, but his hands slap on the wood above my head, caging me in with his body. "Where do you think you're going, Snow?"

"I'm going to help him."

"He's being helped."

I whirl and narrow my eyes at him, frustrated at his words and how messed up everything is. "He sounds like he's on the brink of death, and you're sitting here all glib."

"You don't have the full story, and you're not ready for it."

"You don't get to tell me what I am or am not ready for, Lorne. You're not my fucking keeper."

My knee connects with his balls, forcing him to stumble back. I open the door and run toward Declan's tortuous screams.

CHAPTER 22

Caspian

I like to torture people. I get hard at the sight of blood. But I fucking hate doing this. Neither Lorne nor Declan gets the toll this shit takes on me. I had to fucking leave him here and take a shower because my head was so messed up, and I was afraid I'd do the kind of damage I couldn't take back.

Crimson falls from Declan's hands, holes puncturing the center of his palms from nails placed there to hold him on the cross.

O Lord Jesus Christ, redeemer and savior, forgive my sins, just as you forgave Peter's denial and those who crucified you. Count not my transgressions but rather my tears of repentance. Remember not my iniquities but my sorrow for the offenses I have committed against you. I long to be true to your word and pray that you will love me and come to make your dwelling place within me. I promise to give you praise and glory in love and service all the days of my life."

The fucking nutter has been praying the whole time. He's getting the shit kicked out of him, screaming in pain, but he keeps repeating that stupid prayer. What he's doing is fucked up, but my hard cock on display is as messed up. The number of times I've beaten his stupid ass and fucked him while he lay on his stomach, beaten and bloody, is too many to count. Just like he needs this, I have to fuck after. Sometimes Lorne will suck my cock as I do this, but that doesn't happen tonight, so it will be me pounding into Declan's ass.

"Please," Declan begs when I stop flogging him. "More. I need more. I'm still thinking about her."

"Fuck this, man. You'd rather fuck yourself up over fucking her." Rage fuels me as I pull my arm back and strike him as hard as possible. "We could be balls deep in perfection instead. I'm here beating your ass, and for what? Because you can't shake what your cunt aunt said to you over ten years ago? I knew you should have been the one to kill her. It should have been you who took that bitch's last breath."

"My hardness of heart toward my neighbor's faults and my readiness to make allowance for my own: O Lord forgive me!"

I drop the whip and rush to him. Blood spurts and splatters on my face as I pull the first nail from his hand. The sickness in me has my cock hard and my tongue slipping out between my lips. I pull his hand to my mouth and lap at his self-inflicted wounds.

"Your fucking sick," a sweet voice calls from the doorway.

Sunshine.

She steps into the room, walks up to the table, and holds up the knife I put there. The one I used on Lorne and didn't have time to clean up before Declan pulled his usual shit. "He's in pain, and instead of helping him, you're taking advantage." Her knuckles go white as she holds the handle of the blood-stained knife with a death grip before she slices the inside of her arm and holds it up to me. "Here, you fucking vampire, take it and leave him alone."

I drop Declan's hand. His arm falls limp while his other hand is still bound to the cross. His head hangs low, and new lash marks cover his body, blanketing those he's attained over the years.

Sunshine steps back with every step I take forward, but she doesn't make it to the door before I'm on her. My fingers dig into her chin as I tilt her head and peer at her. "You think I'm the one who makes him do this? Think I enjoy beating him until he almost bleeds out? You storm in here with the idiotic notion that I enjoy having to peel his body off that and dig the thorns from his forehead as I tend to his wounds? You stand here assuming I haven't spent the last ten years desperate for him to find another venue for his demons other than forcing me to do this?"

I slice my hand on the blade as I pull the knife from her grip.

"What are you doing?"

"Taking my knife back."

She lets go of the handle rapidly, as if it singed her flesh. "You're insane. What if I tugged it back? You could've sliced your hand right off."

"I'd live."

Noelle says nothing; she pushes past me and goes to Declan. Her hands fly to the nail, and she turns her head away as she pulls the steel. Her hands fall and she glares at me. "Help me, damn it. Get him off this thing."

"Why? He'll just be back there the next time his emotions get too much for him."

Chapter 23

Declan

"Why do you do this?"

The sweetest voice I've ever heard. Eve. I picture Angels sounding like her. Perfect.

"Run, Eve. Run before Pandora's box gets you. You're too sweet to be mixed up with us. We'll ruin you. We will drag you down to hell and diminish all your light."

Cas growls at me, a warning. "Shut up, you idiot."

Blood spills from my palm as he pulls out the remaining nail and unties the rope binding my wrists to the cross. The first time he saw me do this, he was upset. Said how I was going to lose my hand because it couldn't support my body weight. He's the one who taught me to tie my wrists with the rope. Cas is not what people see. Sure, he's insane, but when he gives a fuck about you, it's a force. He probably cares more about me than any other human on this planet, yet he's the one I treat the worst.

I'm in the in-between. The void that grips me and makes the pain stop. My body floats with pleasure from the unbelievable pain. At some point, a ritual I partook in to show God my dedication turned into something that helped me function in life.

"What's on his head?" Noelle demands.

Cas scoffs. "A crown of torns. He likes to play up the whole Jesus sacrificial thing."

Soft hands move along my head. I wince at the stinging pain of the crown slowly being removed. The sting of the thorns being plucked from my flesh makes me shiver.

"Where the heck did you get one of these?"

"He made it. Afterward, Lorne destroyed the rose garden."

I remember that day. Lorne got so pissed he took the gasoline to the bushes and set the whole thing on fire.

I was nineteen. It was after the first time I kissed him. He wouldn't look at me for weeks. That made the pain so much worse because I didn't know how to tell him it wasn't because of him but me. That was the day I decided never to kiss Cas. I would not risk hurting another person I loved again, but that decision hurt him, anyway.

They're speaking about me, but I'm not here. I'm having an out-of-body experience. I'm floating and watching a movie. It's not me who's beaten, battered, and bruised. I'm a vessel. My flesh means nothing.

"Do you have a medical kit?"

"Yes."

"Well, go get it."

Cas chuckles. "Who knew a pretty girl bossing me around could get me so hard?"

"What the fuck is wrong with you? Your friend or lover or whatever the heck you all are to each other is lying here disfigured and bleeding, and you're thinking about your penis?"

"Do you honestly want to make him feel better?"

"Of course I do."

"Then get on your knees and suck his cock."

Chapter 24

Caspian

My head snaps back with the force of her open palm slap. "Wrong guy, love. Hitting is his thing, not mine."

Usually, I'd bend over and make her scream my name, but I'm pissed. I don't care so much about her hitting me. I like fucked up, rough sex, and that shit goes part and parcel with my way of life. What has me reeling is that she thinks I do this to him willingly. She had to pick a bad guy and assumed it wa[illegible] Well, if she wants a villain, I'll gladly give her one.

She winces as I roughly grab her wrists and tug her to me. With my other hand, I tilt the blade of the knife to her neck. Her tits rise and fall rapidly, and her pupils dilate. "You'd look pretty with your neck slashed. I'm not into fucking a corpse, but I'll make an exception for one as pretty as you."

I push her back one step at a time, the blade pressing on her jugular. Letting her sense that I could slit her throat and bathe in her blood at any moment. I'd never do it, but I like the fear I sense from her. It's a shot of adrenaline in my veins.

She's wearing one of Lorne's t-shirts. It's too snug and a little too short on me, but on her, it falls mid-thigh. She shivers as I push up the hem, my hands moving up her leg to the apex of her thighs. "You're wet, aren't you, Sunshine? Your sweet cunt is dripping. Bet you'd even let me fuck you with the knife like a good girl."

Her nipples perk and her legs part. I burst out laughing. "Sunshine, why don't you be honest with yourself? You're a good, pious girl who wants to be nothing more than my dirty little whore."

"I don't," she pants.

My fingers slide between her slit and pinch her clit, making her moan. "One set of lips is lying while the others are begging to be forced into submission by my cock. Which should I listen to, Sunshine?"

"You disgust me. All this is deranged."

She jerks as I ram two fingers into her cunt hole while using the blade to rip the shirt from the collar to the hem, exposing her giant tits and mouthwatering stomach. "So deranged, Sunshine. Too bad it's depraved acts that make you so wet."

Her hands aren't pushing me away now. They're on my shoulders, helping her maintain balance. I make a small incision at her navel before moving the knife up between her tits. I circle the tip of the blade along her nipple, and she parts her legs. "Sunshine, you like this, don't you? You like the idea of me gutting you like a fish so long as your greedy cunt is full."

"Please," she begs.

"Please, what?"

"I need to cum."

My lips turn up as I smirk at her. I remove my fingers from her pussy and step back.

Her confused eyes roam my face. "Why did you stop?"

The girl is driving me crazy. I want to bend her over and turn her into a twinkie, to consume her in every way. She's become the essence in my veins, and I hate the idea of ever being without her. "Because I want to see you crawl and beg."

"I'm not getting on my knees for you."

I smile as I glide the blade stained with her blood on my tongue, my eyes not once leaving hers. She can pretend she doesn't get off on this, but how her body reacts lets me know she's lying. I'm just not sure if it's to herself or me.

There is something perverse in making the pure depraved. A rush you get when you see something sweet longing to be dirty. "Not only will you get on your knees for me, Sunshine, but you'll also beg to drown in my cum."

"You're sick. You're all sick."

"That may be, but you're the one craving to be infected by the disease."

She drops her head, shielding her eyes from me. In two steps, I'm in front of her, gripping her long black hair and yanking her head back. "Don't do that. Don't feel shame for something natural. I wave the knife toward Declan's bruised and battered body on the bed. "I already deal with one fucker who can't admit the truth. Whatever you do, Sunshine, don't add to my burden. Because I don't think I can take anymore."

She parts her lips to speak, but I drop the blade and cradle her face in my hands before crushing my lips to hers. "I am fucking done talking."

She tastes pure and warm, and all I want to do is drown in her.

Kissing Noelle is so different from kissing the guys. Where they're hard and bitter, she's soft. With them, I'm an avalanche who doesn't need to hold back, but with her, my desire moves like warm summer rain, comforting and protective.

Her legs wrap around my waist as I lift her. My cock is consumed with the heat radiating from her pussy, but it's not her cunt I want to possess so much as her damn heart.

I pull back, both of us panting as if we've been running for days. Maybe in some ways, we have. I know I sure have been running my entire damn life. I touch my forehead to hers. "Your body can leave me, but I'll haunt you until your dying day. And on that day, I'll plunge a dagger into my heart because a world without you would be utterly bleak. For my only glimmer of light in the darkness would cease to exist."

I slam her body against the wall and cover it with mine like a blanket. Without warning, I shove my cock into her pussy. I don't ask permission because I'm not sure what I would do if she said no, and that makes me an asshole. But I don't care. The desperate need for her is too strong to negotiate with reason. If I had to, I'd chain her up to have her for all eternity. Obsession isn't always instant. It's not like a wall of bricks falling over your head. Sometimes it's subtle and invisible, like the wind. You can't see it, but you can feel it.

"Say you'll stay."

Chapter 25

Lorne

Cas is rarely vulnerable. He isn't the type of man who will split himself open and let someone see the festering wounds under the armor he's built for himself. Out of the three of us, he's the one who lives the most in denial. It's like he's created another realm to protect himself from all the horrendous trauma he's endured.

They haven't even noticed I'm standing here. They're in a world of their own. He cut her. I was wondering how long he'd last before that happened. By the look of the blood at his feet, he's cut her multiple times.

Seems like she didn't complain since she's wrapped around him like a monkey while he slams her body against the wall with the thrust of his hips.

"More. Give me more," she pants.

"You sure you want more, Snow?"

They turn to me. Cas smirks, and she simply nods her head.

"Words, Snow. Use your words."

"Yes," she whimpers.

"Bring her to the bed," I order.

I move toward Declan, who's lying on the bed, stroking his cock as he takes in the show. He has the lube on his nightstand next to the Holy Bible. The irony isn't lost on me. The two things that give Declan both pleasure and torment.

Cas keeps fucking Snow as he carries her to the bed, and by the way she's moaning in ecstasy, she seems to love it.

I pour the lube on Declan's stiff cock and rub it in. I turn to Snow and dip a finger in her ass crack before sliding in and out of her. "We're going to fuck you hard. We're going to fuck you in all your holes, and we're going to watch as you leak our cum for our pleasure. Understand?"

She nods again.

I grip her throat and squeeze until she turns red. "I don't enjoy repeating myself, Snow. I told you once that nodding shit doesn't work for me. Use your words like a big girl."

"Yes," she gasps.

I abandon her throat. "Good girl. You like a finger in your ass, don't you?"

"Yes."

"Well, baby girl, you're about to get a lot more."

She screams in blissful agony as Cas slowly impales her on Declan's cock.

Declan's hands move to her tits and he pulls on her nipples, stretching them until it seems he may rip them off. Snow doesn't object and leans back into him, so I let it go. A part of me thinks maybe that's the attraction for Declan. She seems to get off on pain.

"Choke her, Cas." My order is final. He's already been in her cunt, twice, and this time I'm going to be the one lost in her pussy.

He slides out of her and smirks like a lunatic. "Know what my favorite part of a twinkie is, Sunshine?"

Noelle shakes her head. "No."

"The fuckin' filling. Be a good little fuck toy for us, and I'll reward you with the cleanup."

She laughs as I grip her knees and push my cock into her. I'm not gentle. I don't want to be. My need for her has bubbled and boiled over. As soon as my cock's wrapped up by her wet cunt, a sense of calm comes over me. Some odd notion of home, something I've never experienced before. I don't like it and I love it all at the same time. "What spell have you put us under, Snow?"

She gazes into my eyes, her brown challenging my green. "You're the ones who kidnapped me. I was minding my own—"

She doesn't finish the sentence. Cas's cock is in her mouth. "You talk too much, Sunshine. Sometimes it's better to gobble some cock and get fucked to oblivion."

Chapter 26

Noelle

I am not an insecure woman, but I never thought in a million years I would be the center of a sexy as fuck man fiesta. Sure, the three of them are beyond fucked up, but holy hell, their bodies seem to be carved out of granite. Hard and big. Everywhere. I mean everywhere. Their dicks are so long and thick that I fear they'll rip me apart, but they hurt in the best possible way.

Declan grips my sides, which should have mad[illegible] self-conscious because of my rolls, but the way [illegible] cradles me makes me feel like I belong on the big screen. I feel powerful, sexy, and desired.

"Fuck, you're hot. Bounce on our cocks, Snow. Jiggle those giant tits and show us you're our good slut."

Cas cradles my face, pushing his cock further into my throat and forcing me to gag. "Such a good cock-sucker, Sunshine. It's like you were born to be face-fucked."

My mouth waters from being too full. I'm not sure how it's humanly possible to get his cock all the way down my throat, but Cas is sure trying. "Be a good slut for Daddy and relax your throat. You're gonna be a good girl and take it all for me."

Cas fists my hair, holding my head in a firm yet loving manner before he rams his cock all the way in. I try to cough to ease the fear of choking, but it's as if he doesn't notice my struggle for air. He pushes in so far that my nose presses against his rock-hard lower abs. "You want to breathe, Sunshine?"

I try to speak, but my "yes" is muffled, so I nod.

"Then you better make me cum as quickly as possible."

Oh god, he's not joking. These three men kill for a living. Fear courses through me as I evaluate the situation. As good as all this is, do I want to risk death for carnal bliss?

Intrusive thoughts of death by dicking leave my brain as hands squeeze my breasts. At first, my nipples are tweaked gently, but then the pain becomes unbearable. My ass and pussy are on fire, but in the best way. The pain has dissipated, and now a surge of pleasure rocks my core. A finger on my clit, slow, methodical circles, making me want to float away. Pressure builds in my stomach, wanting to burst into a kaleidoscope of unadulterated bliss.

"That's it, Snow, keep gripping my dick. Our pretty girl wants to come like a fucking whore for us, doesn't she?"

God, his mouth. I did not know being talked to like this would be so damn erotic.

"Fuck, I'm going to cum down your pretty little throat. I don't want you to swallow, Sunshine. Hold it in your mouth for me like a good slut. Daddy likes pretty little whores to do as they're told."

Cas holds my head down and unleashes blasts of hot cum into my mouth. I try not to swallow, but it's like drowning. "It's a big load, baby. You're doing well. Keep as much as you can in your mouth for me."

With a final grunt and thrust of his hips, Cas pumps the last few drops of cum into my mouth and slowly pulls out from my lips. "You deserve a reward for being such a good girl."

Fireworks. All I see are fireworks. I've masturbated and made myself cum many times, but nothing, and I mean nothing, has ever been like this. It's as if his tongue is some sort of accelerant—one flick and kaboom.

"Fuck," Declan groans as his cum disperses in my ass, followed by a rapid thrust from Lorne and his release.

Cas appears in front of me, his dick hard again. "Hope you were a good girl and kept your mouth full of my cum, Sunshine."

I nod, unable to speak for fear my mouth will leak saliva and cum.

Cas smirks as he yanks my head back. "Show me."

I open my mouth and almost choke at the vast amount of liquid tipped to the back of my throat.

"Such a perfect, pretty whore. I'm gonna get underneath you, and I want you to let it slip between your lips and fall down your body for me." He hits Declan's thigh. "Get the fuck up, Declan."

Get up? The guy's mangled. I'm surprised he could have sex. If sex is this good when his body is broken, I can only imagine how he'd rock my world in top form. But of all that, I'm the most grateful that

Declan doesn't look like he's in pain. He doesn't seem sad. So perhaps all this is the best thing for him.

Declan grabs my sides and slides me off him but holds me in mid-air. I'm unsure what he's doing until Cas's smug face pops up between my legs. "Ready for that reward, Sunshine?"

"Reward?" Oh, baby Jesus. Please, no more fucking. I'm not sure I can take it.

"Let's see that cum trickle from your face."

I open my lips, and the cum slides down my chin and from the sides of my mouth. It's utterly humiliating and powerful all at once. I'm doing something depraved, but Cas looks at me as if I've shown him the meaning of life. There's a power in a man looking at you as if you're priceless art when you're being degraded. Maybe that's why I'm not running for the hills because even though these three men are depraved in every sense of the word, they make me feel irreplaceable.

His hands grip my hips, and with one solid pull, my vagina is directly on his tongue. Oh, my god. His tongue. It has to be illegal for someone to do these tricks.

He lifts me by my ass so I'm hovering above his face. "Push it all out for me, Sunshine. Give me every drop."

"I can't do that."

"Sure you can. Daddy is hungry, and you're going to be a good girl and feed him."

I gaze at two hungry sets of eyes, one green and one steel gray, staring at my pussy and Cas's extended tongue.

Lorne smiles, his hand on his dick. "You look beautiful, Snow. Give the man what he wants."

The tip of Cas's nose is against pussy, and the tip of his tongue is pressed against my ass.

Panic. Sheer panic as he moves his tongue to my ass as soon as he's done with my vagina. "What are you doing?"

"I cleaned your sweet pussy," he mumbles. "Now I'm going to suck every drop of cum out of your big, sexy ass."

My body stiffens as I push the cum out, and Cas's tongue delves into my anus. At first, I'm too nervous to enjoy it, but soon my head falls back, and I grind my pussy and ass on his face and tongue. Between his wicked tongue and its taboo nature, I'm back in the realm of utter bliss.

"That's it, Snow. Let it all go. Show us how you long to be our dirty slut."

Chapter 27

D eclan

I've been up for hours, one of those spent under scalding water, hoping the pain of my scars will quench my thirst to suffer for existing.

The silent darkness of night does two things. It shields the wicked and awakens desire. As I sit here, my eyes wander between a bible I fear and respect and the three people I crave so much I'd be willing to burn in damnation.

Life is a mean bitch with a sick sense of hu
Choices that make us happy in the mortal realm
the same ones that cause us the most harm in th

afterlife. But in the stillness, sunsets and rainbows flood my mind, and for a moment, I conceive that it's okay to be happy in this world with no thought of what's coming in the next.

My eyes linger on Noelle. She's nestled between Cas and Lorne. They're her shelter and the storm. I don't understand how she's come to mean so much to not one but all of us in such a short time.

But isn't that the meaning of a miracle, a phenomenon that you can't explain? It simply is. She is much like a prophet, a message of hope, absolution, and redemption sent to sinners by God to guide them.

She creates an adhesive that holds the frail fabric of our sanity intact. Even in moments of pure lust-filled rage, I sense peace when I'm with her. But as much as I want to keep her and how desperately I need her, I know we'll destroy her.

I place the bible on the nightstand and head into the washroom. The glare of the warm white light magnifies the new wounds on my body. I scrub my face with my bandaged hands. A reminder of how fucked up I truly am. The horror she must have felt when she walked into the room and saw me, the sheer bewilderment and shock that likely coursed through her body.

Before I can stop myself, my hand connects with the mirror, creating a fractured spider. I laugh as I gaze at the dispersed lines. The fragments are much like my mind—the source of trauma in the center and twisted lines around it. My destruction was forged in the womb. I never had a chance.

"Declan?"

I shut my eyes. Even in my waking hours, her voice still haunts me. I grip the belt lying on the counter and wrap it around my hand before I strike my back. "Loving Lord Jesus, for too long have I kept you out of my life. I accept that I am a sinner and cannot save myself."

"Declan." Her voice lingers, refusing to leave me.

My knuckles are white as I hold on to the edge of the counter, bracing myself as I strike again. "Lord, no longer will I shut the door when I hear you knocking."

"Declan!" This time, she screams right before the lash of the belt and the sound of a thump.

I close my eyes and focus on my retribution. I desperately try to push anything else out of my mind other than my undying need for God.

My hand is steady as I throw the belt in mid-air, but there's no sting from the leather on my back. I tug, and this time the belt seems heavier.

"No, Declan. I won't let you hurt yourself."

I whirl, and standing before me is a vision. My Eve.

"The effects of last night haven't healed. Look at your hand, Declan."

I gaze at my palm and see blood seeping from the wound. "It doesn't matter. This is just a vessel for my spirit. I don't need to save a shell. The penance is for my soul."

She tugs at the belt. "I won't let you. The god I love wouldn't want you to do this. My god is loving, he is kind, and he is merciful. Whatever deity you're harming yourself for doesn't give a fuck about you. You're not the judge of humanity and the ruler over what's pious and sinful."

"Let me?" I laugh, circling my hand on the belt and pulling her toward me. "How cute that you think you're a match for me." My hand circles her throat.

Fear flashes in her eyes, but she holds her ground, her shoulders back. "I'm not scared of you."

I slam her against the wall, holding her tightly by her throat. Her hands grip the vise of my fingers, desperate to pull them off her as her skin turns a reddish hue. "There's only one person you should fear, Eve, and that's your maker, not me, my sweet Jezebel. I'm only a fucking executioner."

Her naked pussy is now level in the air with my cock. I don't ask permission. I don't whisper sweet nothings. I just rail into the warmth of her cunt, hoping to chase away my demons.

I release her neck, and her hands replace mine. I'm not sure if it's as a shield or a bandage against the damage I've already inflicted and will continue to as long as she's near me.

I bend her back until her head touches the marble floor. I support her waist with one hand while the other lashes her skin with the leather. "If I can't drive the demon out of myself, I'll fuck it out of you."

She places her hands at the sides of her head to aid in holding her weight. She should run, but she doesn't. Instead, she bites down on her lip and moans, taking the lashes of penance meant for me.

"Flee from sexual immorality. All other sins a person commits are outside the body, but whoever sins sexually sins against their own body."

"Stop quoting scripture, Declan. Stop twisting everything you do and making it seem like you're acting by the will of God. If you want to fuck me, fuck me. If you long to debase me, do it. Don't wear faith as a mask to cover up your depravity. Be a man and take responsibility."

My vision blurs with the rage festering in my veins. A part of me wants her to suffer for how I react to her, but another part wants to burn for what I'm doing to her. I'm unable to forge my emotions into words, which fuels the fires of rage within me. All I know how to do is pray and draw blood. I wanted it to be mine, but she wouldn't leave.

She screams as the tip of the leather belt connects with her nipple.

"Humble yourselves, therefore, under God's mighty hand, that He may lift you in due time."

I drop the belt and grip her hips, pinching her flesh as I propel her on my cock. My thrusts are wild and untamed. "How does it feel, Eve, to be nothing but a fucking cum dump? To be used like a piece of meat? That's all you whores deserve."

"You forget, Declan. It was a common whore who stood by Jesus when the men who claimed to be apostles abandoned him. Call me a whore, spit the word out like it's poison, but you know the truth as well as I do. It was the whore and the Madonna. Two sides to the coin for true believers."

She squeals, in pain or delight, I'm not sure as I lift her ankles and fuck her like she's a blow-up doll. I want to drown her in my cum, use her, and love her.

My emotions fester with nowhere to go but to be unleashed on her. She's different from Lorne and Cas because I view them as comrades and fellow soldiers. They don't threaten me because they're broken like me.

But Noelle is a threat to everything I believe is true. She's a mirror showing me a reflection I can't bear. She's the balm that can soothe my soul, but I'm the venom that will be her undoing.

I tug her body up, circling her in my arms and pulling her tightly to me, wanting to lose myself in her warmth. I bury my face in her long dark hair and inhale her scent, imprinting it in my memory forever. "You can't stay. We'll destroy you. I'll demolish your light and leave you a vacant shell. Run, Eve. Run because nothing good lies within our depths."

Three Months Later

Chapter 28

Lorne

She didn't return for our parents' wedding. I thought she'd come back then, and I'd have her. But the day came, and as I searched the crowd for her long black hair, all my hopes vanished into smoke.

The first month Snow was gone, we wallowed in our misery and blamed Declan. Cas punished him, mostly. He got creative and started learning how to put intricate lash marks on his back with a flogger and a cane. Declan took it, both out of guilt and his own sick needs. I shut him out, wouldn't talk to him, glance at him, or touch him. I couldn't bear the sight of him.

Then I began hating myself for causing him pain. I realized I was adding to the fucked up shit in his head, and that was something I never wanted to do. That's when my anger toward him was redirected into finding Snow.

Edward was useless. As much as I asked about her, he always kept his answers vague. One thing is for certain—the man might be ruthless, but he was pure mush for his little girl. She asked him to stay quiet, and he did it with no questions asked.

All I knew was she got into school in Paris. So I began searching, but there was no one by the name of Noelle White registered anywhere.

I'm at the tenth school and once again I've struck out. I flip the collar of my black coat and walk out of the registrar's office into the chill. Pulling my phone out of my pocket, I dial Cas's number to inform him of another dead end, and that's when she appears like a fucking prophecy. I end the call and light a cigarette as I stalk her like an animal watching its prey.

She's a vision. Her head falls back in laughter at the person behind her. My blood runs cold as he flings his arm around her, and she puts her head on his shoulder.

Who the fuck is this guy, and why is he touching what's mine?

I want to bend her over right here and fuck her for the world to see. To lay my claim and mark her so no other man will look at her. Then I want to cum all over that little fucker's smug face so he knows who she belongs to.

I jog to her side of the courtyard, ensuring she doesn't see me. They seem awfully chummy. She's a little too comfortable with him. They pass down the busy sidewalks, so lost in what the other has to say that they barely realize there's a world around them until they stop in front of a cathedral.

Snow swings her arms around him and places a kiss on his cheek before leaving him to enter the gothic building. The venom coursing in me at her lips on his cheek is so strong that I crush the cigarette in my hand, singeing my fingers with the embers before following her inside.

She's already kneeling, hands clasped together, head bowed before an altar. Maybe this is what Declan sees in her—another sucker, just like him.

I grab another smoke and let it dangle from my mouth, not yet lighting it. Uncertain about what to do. I usually have a plan. There is a method to every move I make, but with Noelle, all the planning seems to go out the window. With her, everything I do is on impulse, and that can't be trusted because all my instincts are screaming at me to bend her over and fuck her until she submits.

I approach her and sit in the pew directly behind her. My fingers itch to brush against her hair. My body is tense at having her so close after months of torture, and my cock throbs with the need to bury itself in paradise.

"Aren't imaginary friends a little weird to have at your age?"

Chapter 29

Noelle

I jolt at his voice. A voice I've longed for the last few months. A voice I wished I'd never hear again. My emotions for the three men I left behind are turbulent: fear, anger, love, compassion, and hope, all colliding and fighting for domination.

"What are you doing here?"

Lorne's hand grips my throat, pushing me back so I'm peering up at him. "We've been searching for you, Snow. The hunt for happiness led me to you."

I thought I'd moved on, put the past and the three men who haunt my dreams behind me. But as I stare into his emerald green eyes, I realize I was lying to myself. "Did you consider that I didn't want to be found?"

"Belongings don't get a say about where they're placed. You, my pretty little Snow, belong with us."

"I crossed the Atlantic to get away from you."

"You can hide, and we will seek. You can run, and we will chase. There isn't a place on earth where you don't belong to us."

"That's the problem. You want ownership. I'm not chattel. You can't buy me. I'm a human being."

"This isn't a one-way transaction. We also belong to you. I don't put a lot of faith in superstition or things I can't see, but I'm sure about this. I'm sure about us."

Lorne releases my neck, and I immediately miss his touch. I can't explain my emotions, even to myself. Perhaps I'm too scared. "I like the simplicity of my life here in Paris. I'm not Edward White's daughter. I'm not Lorne Miller's plaything. I'm not Declan Bridges' damnation, and I'm not Caspian Charming's target."

"You're also not Edward White's joy, Lorne Miller's heart, Declan Bridges' Salvation, and Caspian Charming's aim. Snow, if you want to live in France, we'll move here."

"You can't pack up and leave. It's a complicated life in the syndicate."

Lorne laughs. "Our Daddy can take care of business back home."

My head snaps up and I glare at him.

"I was sad not to see you at the wedding, sis."

"No, you weren't."

"You're wrong." Lorne slides into the pew beside me. A ring of smoke floats from his mouth into the cathedral before it morphs and disperses. "Praying for someone to come save you from the sinners?"

"You can't smoke in here. It's the house of God."

He laughs, his eyes on the cross before us, and the depiction of Jesus crucified on it. "If sky daddy didn't want me to get the vice, maybe he shouldn't have created it."

"Seriously, what's your problem with faith? It's not like it's hurting anyone."

"Correction, Snow. It hurts everyone. If it was a benevolent thing someone did and kept to themselves, I wouldn't have a problem. But it's not. Organized religion is used to coerce, pervert and maintain a vacuum for the sheep. Bow your head and keep praying while those with power hurt you. I'm not willing to be a lamb for them to slaughter."

"I'm not hurting anyone!" I scream.

My voice echoes through the cathedral. I'm frustrated. Not in Lorne's lack of belief. I don't care about that because, unlike Declan, my view of God is good. God isn't vengeful to me. God is patient, forgiving, and, most of all, loving.

"Correction again. You're hurting yourself with the notion there will be a guiding light from fantasy. May as well be on your knees asking for dragons to come save you." He smirks, draping his arm around my shoulder before he brings his lips to my ear. "I like the idea of fucking you here. I promise to show you heaven."

What is it about this man? He doesn't even have to touch me, and I'm instantly aroused. Three months in Paris and I couldn't get excited by any guy here, but all Lorne has to do is exist and I'm gushing like Niagara. "I hate you."

"Snow, you don't hate me. You hate that your pretty pink cunt is gushing for me."

"That's what I hate the most, that my body wants to bend for you, leaving my heart tattered on the ground. You have women throwing themselves at you. Go fuck one of them and leave me in peace. I don't want your head games and mind-blowing sex. I want something more."

"Women may throw themselves at me, but you're the only woman who'll ever have me. I know we call you a cum dump, but we don't mean it. It's all part of the sex play. Part of our devotion to you, because you're fuckin' everything, Snow. You're not a fuck. You're life itself."

I want to believe him so badly. To know without a doubt that he means it. That he truly cares for me. "If I mattered that much, you'd open up to me. You only want to give me bits and piece with the mind-blowing sex."

"The sex is pretty fucking spectacular, isn't it?"

"A relationship can't survive on sex alone. I need more."

Lorne remains silent, his eyes on the altar. "What do you want to know?"

"For starters, why do you have those burn marks on your skin? Why does Cas hurt himself and why is Declan in so much pain?"

He nods. "I can only give you one of those three. It's not as horrifying as the other two tales you seek, but it's my truth, and I can only share my story." He pauses to draw a breath. "I killed my dad and took his power. But I didn't kill him for his position in life. I killed him because of who he was. My father enjoyed two things: fire and children, and both were for twisted reasons. My father was a pedophile. He ran one of the biggest sex rings on the planet because he craved children and wanted to make sure he had a steady supply."

My emotions are like a light switch; on for anger and off for sad. I want to dig up Angelo Miller's grave and burn him up all over again. But I'm also heartbroken because I can sense where this is going.

"He liked to get me to burn the kids. It turned him on. That's how I met Cas."

Tears spring down my face in waves. My boys. My beautiful boys.

Lorne laughs, but there's no humor in it. "Cas was probably his biggest mistake. He was the one who gave me courage. He bit my father's dick off and spat it in his face. Angelo didn't know what hit him. He screamed at me to get someone, but Cas just looked at me and calmly asked if I had any accelerant."

"Lorne." My voice emerges as a strangled whisper.

He grips my wrist as I lift my hand to his face and growls, "Don't do that. Don't feel sorry for me. I'm not helpless. I went through shit. Everyone goes through shit. Two people I love more than life have gone through much worse."

"I don't pity you, Lorne. I want to comfort you because I care about you. I'm glad you killed him. Did ... Did he ever touch you?"

"Did he fuck me? No. I was there to torture. He made me watch. I'd get hard, and I assumed I was a sick fuck like him. Cas was the first kid he tried to get me to burn. He liked to burn me while he made the other kids"—his Adam's apple bobs as he pushes his palms into his eyes—"do things. Horrible things."

I want to hug him, to cradle him in my arms and love him. To show him he deserves better.

"Sometimes, he'd put me in a choke hold and cut off my airway. Occasionally, I'd pass out. But the worst part was that I thought I liked it. It wasn't until Cas that I understood my physical reaction didn't constitute consent."

Suddenly, he jumps off the pew bench, his expression distraught. "Jesus! Fuck! Did we rape you?"

He falls to his knees in front of me, his head buried in my lap. "I'm sorry, Snow. I'm so sorry. We have a hard time with it all. We can't grasp what's okay and isn't.

But you were making it better. I could see it. The fucked up thing is that I can't even promise it won't happen again. Jesus, no wonder you ran away."

"Don't apologize for something you don't believe you did wrong. You can sit here and say sorry, but you don't mean it. The truth is, I didn't say no then and I won't now. Or ever."

He rises, his gaze searching mine. "I need you." The words are full of longing and desperation.

He grabs my nape and tugs me to the floor. My hands work as if on autopilot, unbuckling his belt and lowering the zipper of his navy wool dress pants to unleash his mammoth cock.

He grips his girth with one hand, slapping me in the face with it. "Be a good girl for your new brother and open wide."

This is obscene. We're in a place of worship. This is sacrilegious and wrong in so many ways. But I want it. I want him to know that I want it. That he isn't a monster to me. He's something more, something better. My lips part and the taste of pre-cum lands on my tongue before he forces his entire cock into my mouth.

"Well, what do we have here?"

I'm startled by Cas's voice. I try to pull away from Lorne, but I can't because his hand is at the back of my head, pushing my nose against his pelvis. The tip of his cock is down my esophagus, and I can't breathe. He's going to kill me. I left and people don't leave men like him. This is his retribution.

"Just showing our sweet little Snow what happens when she's a bad girl and runs from us."

From the corner of my eye, I watch Cas. He's holding a knife. The edge of the blade shimmers and he's smiling. But it's not his usual cocky smirk. He looks sinister, like he's done playing games, and is on a mission.

"Hello, Sunshine. Miss me?"

Chapter 30

Caspian

She's a deer caught in headlights, and that makes my cock hard as fuck for her.

She stumbles back from Lorne, her eyes never leaving me. I take a step forward and she takes a step back.

Lorne steps to me, his cock still hanging out. "Take it easy, Cas. Don't spook her."

I point my blade to his chest. "Spook her? She's lucky I don't carve my name on her whole damn ch punishment. She fucking ran off. We didn't k where she was, or if she was safe." I step forward a slide the shiny wrapped present along the pew toward her. "I brought you a gift, Sunshine. Open it."

Her hands shake as she pulls the bow off and rips the paper.

"A box that size was a bitch to find. Apparently, they're only supposed to only hold delicate jewelry. But I know a guy and he came through in a pinch."

She gazes at me before she lifts the top of the red velvet box and screams. "You're fucking crazy!"

The box drops from her hand, and a perfect human heart rolls down the aisle and right under my feet.

"Why don't you come here and give me a kiss?"

"This is a church, Cas!" she cries.

I smirk. "Can't think of a better place for a holy union. Declan's on a job, but if he was here, you'd have yourself a holy trinity. I'm not gonna tell you again, Sunshine. Get your big, sexy ass over here, right now."

She rises, and for a second, I think she's going to do as she's told. But then she runs.

"Oh, Sunshine!" I call. "That was a terrible thing you just did. I was going to reward you for being a good girl, but it seems you'd rather be my bad little slut." I turn to Lorne. "I love a good hunt."

I chase after her while Lorne adjusts his pants. I feel a little bad that I stopped his face fucking session, but this will be worth it.

"This is a church, Cas. People could walk in any moment!" she yells. "Trust me, you don't want to fuck me right now."

"Of course I do, Sunshine. I would fuck you twenty-four-seven if your pussy could handle it."

"No, you don't. I'm on my period."

I drop the knife and practically fly over the pew until she's trapped in my arms. "Oh, Sunshine, you just threatened me with a good time."

I don't wait for her to reply. I yank her pants down and shove her back, pulling out her tampon and tossing it behind me. Pushing her knees apart, I press my nose against her cunt and inhale the sweetest scent I've ever come across. Sunshine's bloody cunt.

Chapter 31

Noelle

Every muscle in my body tenses. I'm mortified. I'm not sure what I should do because the idea of having someone's face between my thighs while Aunt Flow is in town isn't the most comforting notion.

I jolt as Cas slaps my pussy. "Can you fucking relax?" His head peers up in between my legs. "Can a man eat in fucking peace?"

"I'm not sure this will be good for you."

"Lorne, shove your cock in her mouth. She's talking too much again."

Lorne glides the tip of his cock along my lips, "Open wide, sis. Big brother wants to give you a present."

Why is that hot? He's not my brother. My dad married his mom five minutes ago, but the words are so damn filthy that I might come. My mouth falls open and Lorne glides between my lips. Giving a blow job upside down is interesting.

"You know what, Noelle? A good fuck is what you need. You think too much. Always stuck in your head." Lorne grips my throat with his tattooed hands, holding me firmly as he pushes his cock to the back of my throat.

My nose hits his balls. I can't breathe, but I don't care because Cas's tongue on my pussy would be a fantastic way to die.

I wrap my legs around his neck, holding his head firmly between my legs. His large hands grip my ass, pulling my pussy closer to his face. So close that I wouldn't be surprised if he suffocated.

Cas's tongue moves to my opening as his thumb and forefinger pinch my clit. My body stiffens and feels like Jell-O at the same time. Cas moans as my thighs tighten around him. I can't hold on anymore.

Lorne pulls out of me, and saliva falls from my mouth as I gasp for breath. He bends and places a punishing kiss on my lips. "Little Snow," he murmurs.

My eyes close. I'm lost, consumed by Cas's tongue. Time stops and I'm transported elsewhere, somewhere tempting and treacherous.

My eyes flash open as pain shoots through me. Crimson gleams from Lorne's mouth. He smiles as his fingers glide along my lips. "There. Now your lips are red as blood."

With those words that should place nothing but fear in my heart, I close my eyes and come.

Chapter 32

Lonre

Cas lifts his head and stands. He looks ridiculous. His face is covered in blood, and he's sporting a goofy grin like a child who's outsmarted a parent to get what he wants.

"From now on, when you get your period, you'll sleep in my bed. I'd also like it if you free bleed. You can stay in my room, and I'll get anything you need. You only have to keep your legs open and let me tongue fuck that bloody cunt all day."

Noelle bolts up. *"What?* That's seriously messed up. What's wrong with you?"

She moans as Cas dips his finger into her pussy, holding her in place. "Is that a serious question, Sunshine? There's plenty wrong with me, but eating you out on your rag isn't one of them. And from the way you gushed on my face, you liked it."

Noelle covers her face with her hands and groans. I don't want her to suffer any shame about anything she likes or that we do to her. The three of us grew up with so much shame that it festered and turned into something dark and depraved. I refuse to have my Snow feel that way. I won't let our sickness touch her. She is the antidote to the poison surging in our veins. The one person on this planet who takes away the bitterness, the anger, and the pain.

Cas slaps her pussy, and she yelps. "There's no way any woman has felt a tongue on her pussy during her period and considers it dirty. Sunshine, it's not my fault that most men are too stupid to worship their women like queens. You should consider yourself lucky that isn't the case for you."

I abandon her face, and she takes a moment to gather her senses. She won't run. She's naked from the waist down and her pants are on the floor.

"You know," she says, her eyes cast down to her hands, "I assumed this would be Declan's thing, not the two of you."

"Declan's lucky to be alive," I rasp.

Her head shoots up, and her eyes search my face frantically. "What's wrong? Where is he? Is he okay?"

Cas chuckles. "Why do you care?"

Snow's black cotton panties are in her hand as she moves it back and forth like a granny waving her finger. "You don't control if Declan comes near me. I might succumb to your insanity and fuck the three of you, but none of you ever get to tell me I cannot be with the other. GOT IT?"

Cas crosses his arms in a display of sheer cockiness. The human equivalent of a peacock fanning out its feathers. "Thought you didn't want us, Sunshine."

Noelle steps up to his face, waving her panties by his nose. "Perhaps I don't want *you.*"

Cas's nostrils flare and his jaw ticks before he rips her panties from her hand by his teeth. He lifts the bottom of the garment up to his nose and inhales. "Fuck, these smell good! I'm gonna need you to wear a few pairs for a couple of days for me. I need something to remind me of home when I'm out on jobs."

He tucks the panties in the pocket of his jeans and smirks. He gently glides a finger along her jaw, trailing it along her face before he slams her down on the floor, his hand tightly wound around her throat. "I'm gonna say this once, so you listen nice and good, Sunshine. You don't want Daddy to punish you for not learning your lesson the first time. I would bleed out from the most gruesome torture for you." He grabs onto his cock and balls. "I'd cut this off to ensure your wellbeing." She gasps as he pushes three fingers into her pussy. "I love you! But if you think you have a say about how we protect you, you're wrong. So the next time you get smart with me about that topic, I will tie your ass up and fuck this pussy until I permanently turn your brain into mush."

Her eyes bulge as he bends and kisses her. He bites her lips much more viciously than I did. "Make sure you understand, Sunshine, because next time I'll make your other lips bleed."

He moves away and cleans off the fingers from her pussy by dragging them into his mouth and licking his lips. "Fucking delicious."

Snow shuffles back before she runs again.

Cas and I are both on her heels, and she doesn't make it far before I grip her and slam her against the wall with my forearm. "Where do you think you're running off to, Snow? It's not nice to get yours and leave our balls blue."

I grip her hair and tug back. The burning need for her is all-consuming. With Snow, nothing in my mind makes sense. She's the cure and the affliction. The reason and the cause. She's the ocean that can drown me and the life raft desperately needed to save my life. So it's not shocking that my desire for her is both pure and corrupted. Sane and demented. Safe and volatile.

There are moments when I want to treat her like delicate silk, and times like this where I want to destroy her because she's decimated me.

"I'm going to fuck you so damn hard that you'll think I've ripped your tight little pussy part. I'm going to pound into this sweet cunt until my balls get tight and I can't think straight. And to be honest, Snow, I don't care if you want it or not."

She cries out as I shove my cock in her. "What's fascinating, Snow, is that I like it when you cry. I get hard because it hurts you. Perhaps it's my upbringing, or maybe it's because the blood of the monster who created me runs rampant in my veins. Does it scare you or turn you on to know that your new brother will take your body whenever and wherever he wants, and there's nothing you can do about it?"

Chapter 33

Noelle

Shame floods my mind as a pool or wetness floods my core. As much as I may long for Lorne to debase me, I also refuse to give up control without a fight. This isn't a fight for sexual domination, it's a battle to see who has more control. For a man like Lorne, all this is contrary to what he's taught. To Lorne, relinquishing control is a loss of power, something he was taught to combat from a young age as if his life depended on it.

But for me, a relationship isn't about who's on top and who remains at the bottom, it's about a balance that creates stability. So as he's fucking me against a wall to solidify his dominance, I will revel in the knowledge that I'm the only one who creates my utopia or brings about my hell.

My lungs expand and I brace myself as I peer up at the intricate woodwork layered in the arches of the cathedral.

I bite down on his neck, sucking his skin as my teeth penetrate his flesh. I'm not gentle. I don't care to be. This man looks at me like I'm a sweet doe. He doesn't yet understand that I can be a lioness. That's the thing about kindness. People view it as a weakness, when it's anything but. There's a strength in being decent, caring for others, and showing compassion. It takes strength to be merciful when all you've witnessed is treachery.

With the flavor of his blood dripping on my tongue, I whisper, "Don't assume you're taking something I haven't given you willingly.

"Look at you, Snow, admitting that behind the good girl demeanor, you're nothing but a filthy whore desperate for her big brother's cock. You turned on by the idea of your stepbrother bending you over and fucking your brains out?"

Heat floods my face, and I gaze at the lights above our heads.

"Tsk, tsk, sis. What would your daddy say if he knew his little girl was getting railed in church like a lowlife street walker?"

I grind my hips, desperate to match every powerful thrust of his hips. "I don't know, big bro. What would your mommy say to you plowing her new daughter up against a wall like an animal?"

Lorne smirks. He lifts me off the wall and tips me back. I brace my hands for the fall, thinking he's about to fuck me the same way Declan did that night.

But before I plummet to the ground, firm hands grip my neck and Cas's hard cock is presented to my mouth. "Open wide, Sunshine."

He plunges into me with force, and as much as I should focus on his movements, I peek under his Ramones T-shirt. Bile rises in my throat, not from his cock being forced down it, but from the etchings on his flesh.

"Fuck, Sunshine, I don't know what's better, your cunt, or your pretty little mouth." He fucks my mouth like it's a sex toy, with no regard to the person attached to the person he's using for his pleasure. My breathing is almost obsolete. "The French do a lot of things right, pastries, sauces, not giving a fuck what anyone thinks of them. But the best thing they ever did was name a fucking orgasm. *Le petite mort.*

Because every time I fuck you, it's like a little death no one else will ever be able to satisfy."

I gasp for breath as he pulls out. He cradles my head in his hand as streams of saliva trail from my mouth. Cas is wrong. *Le petite mort* isn't a little death. The expression is far more complex.

The term expands to mean the brief loss or weakening of consciousness. Because an orgasm makes you feeble. It trips you up and you forget to think logically, which allows you to drive headfirst into something which could be malignant. But the endorphins are so palatable that you don't care how it engulfs you.

Cas gazes at me and the madness always lurking in his eyes has vanished, replaced by tenderness.

"Why do you have so many letters carved into your skin?"

My question is like turning off a light switch. The tender Cas isn't there anymore. The beast returns. He drives his cock into my mouth so hard that I believe I might vomit.

"They're the roadmap of my life, Sunshine. They're the demons I run from and the evil that drives me."

I move a hand to the hem of his T-shirt, slowly lifting the fabric. What I'm doing is like detonating a bomb.

One false move and Cas could explode, taking me with him.

Language has meaning. Words can be a balm to soothe your soul or daggers launched at your heart. So as I read every jagged, healed scar on Cas's chest, it rips my heart into tatters. Whore. Ungrateful. Idiot. Loser. Slut. Cum dump. Worthless.

Tears stream down my face and then I see it. *Property of Sunshine.* The only words that haven't scabbed over and healed. The only words fresh on his pelvis with an arrow pointing to his dick.

Cas grips my neck, picking up his pace, and he lodges his cock more viciously in my mouth. "Sunshine, the only time I want to make you cry is when you're gagging on my cock."

His thrusts are punishing and soothing, a contradiction like the man himself. I drop the hem of his shirt and let it fall above my forehead as I grip his ass for support and lose myself in my body, being fully controlled by these men.

"Be a good girl and take every drop." He holds my face down, my nose directly on the arrow carved into his flesh. He groans and unleashes in waves in the back of my throat.

Lorne grips my hips, his grunts sounding more like a beast than a man. He pulls me to him. "I'm going to fill this pretty cunt, Snow. I'm going to fuck you raw for the rest of our lives and drown you in cum."

His fingers move to my clit, and he rotates the pad of his thumb. Fuck, this man knows his way around a woman's vagina. I moan as my body once again comes for him as if on demand.

"Get over here, Lorne, Hold her shoulders," Cas demands.

Lorne grips beneath my arms and hoists me up while Cas grips my ass, leveling it with his mouth. "Cum and blood. There's nothing better."

His mouth is on me as he laps with abandon. Cas devours me like he's never going to have another meal. It's wild, untamed, and completely feral. Once again, my body is spun tight into a fevered frenzy until I come undone in waves of ecstasy.

"Fuck, Sunshine. This damn pussy."

Lorne places me on the pew and turns to Cas. He grips his cock and points it toward him. "You're not done yet."

Cas winks, a devilish glint in his eyes, and falls to his knees. His hand grips Lorne's balls as his lips slide over his semi-hard, blood-stained dick.

I sit, eyes glued on two of the three men I love, and my heart aches for the third. "I want to see Declan."

Chapter 34

Declan

The sun can heal and harm you. Get too close and get burned. Don't get enough and you'll fall ill from lack of vitamin D. Cas calls her Sunshine because Noelle is a warmth he's never known.

Snow is pure. It covers the dead like a blanket for them to bloom into something beautiful. Lorne's nickname for her because Noelle provides him with hope.

Eve, the woman Adam loved so much that he betrayed God to see her happy. I call her Eve because I fear I'll abandon it all and burn in all eternity just to have her close.

She has an easy way about her with Cas and Lorne, but with me, it's like a brick wall is between us. She can barely look at me, her eyes cast down, staring at the apple tart she's taken a bite of, two of at most.

We've been sitting here for an hour and other than "hello" there have been no words exchanged between us.

My instincts rage at me to flip her over the table and fuck her senseless while the entire restaurant watches. But I don't want to do more damage than I've already done. When I told her to run that night, I meant it, but I didn't know the void and self-destruction it would propel within me.

I grip Lorne's leg. He turns to me and nods before he rises from his chair and I take his place beside her. Lorne's comforting. He knows what I need before I even ask. He's the first person who offered me a sense of safety.

I gaze at Cas. He saved me. I'll never be able to thank him for the five years he sacrificed in jail for protecting me. He's what I needed because I was too weak then. I'm probably just as debilitated now. The worst part is that out of everyone, I've hurt him the most. Kept him at arm's length and made him feel like the outsider looking in. Yet no matter what I've done to him, how I've shoved him away, he's always been there. A rock I can lean on no matter what.

"I have trust issues with women. You're the first woman I've ever been with."

Her fork clangs loudly as it hits her plate. She turns her stunned face to me.

I raise a finger, needing to get everything out before she speaks. "The night I told you to run is the biggest regret of my life, and I have many. It all started with my mother and grew stronger under the guardianship of her sister. My mom came from a middle-class family. Her mother was a nurse, and my grandfather was a teacher. A regular family. Nothing special or extraordinary. Then my mother fell in love with the wrong guy. He had three things; good looks, danger, and he made my grandparents crazy. She took one look at my father, burned her average family to the ground, and ran off with him. He quickly got her addicted to drugs and then knocked her up. I was the product."

I flinch as her hand covers mine. She quickly goes to remove it, but I grab it, intertwining my fingers with hers. "I'm sorry. I'm trying to work on this, and I don't want to hurt you. It's a woman's touch. I don't have any good examples of it."

She nods and offers me a sweet smile.

"I spent the first three years of my life surrounded by drug addicts, prostitutes, and criminals. They didn't sexually abuse me, and they weren't violent, but they were neglectful. But in all honesty, my first three years with them, sitting in my shit for days on end, was better than the hell it would force me into for the next fifteen years."

I glance at the empty tables surrounding us, grateful that Lorne bought out the whole place for the night. This is a conversation I did not want to have with wandering eyes and ears. "I've said none of this out loud before. So I'm not sure what to say or even how to say it."

Noelle glances at Cas and Lorne.

"My parents died of a heroin overdose when I was three. Social services took me in, and it turned out my mother had one living relative, her older sister, who had become a nun. I'm not sure why my aunt took me in. But she tried to exercise my demons out of me."

Noelle gasps, and her hand shoots up to her mouth. "What did she do to you?"

"My aunt considered me a sinner, and sinners needed to be punished in order to be saved. She worked tirelessly to cast my demons out."

A tear slips from her eye. “Three-year-olds don’t have demons. They’re innocent.”

I sigh because my dick is hard. Her showing me sympathy makes me want to hurt her. I did the right thing when I told her to run. I’m doing the selfish thing now, forcing her to stay. But I don’t care anymore. The three months without her were hell. I’ve never known pain so intense in my life, and I’d rather forsake God than forsake her.

“Children aren’t born innocent. We are all sinners, Eve. My aunt didn’t view me as a regular child. I represented an abomination, the spawn of Satan, because my father didn’t just steal her sister. That one union between my parents caused my grandmother to kill herself and my grandfather to become an alcoholic. To my aunt, a living byproduct of all the tests God had put her through, correcting me meant she’d done God’s work.”

Noelle pushes off her chair and whips her hands away from me. Her entire body shakes, and she balls her hands into fists. “Fuck that. You were a baby. You were an innocent baby forced into the world to incompetent pieces of shit. Did she show you how to hurt yourself, Declan? Was she thc useless monster who taught a child how to whip himself because he was unfortunate enough to be born into a cruel world?”

"She tried to do the best she could."

China jumps as Cas slams his fist on the table. "Fuck you, Dec. Fuck you for still making excuses for that cunt after all these years. I was there, Declan. I was there when my father was talking to that perverted priest that your bitch of an aunt worshiped. She knew. She must have. All those boys they traded, all the abuse. I'll never forget that day. The sound of the whip cracking on your back. How you screamed in agony. That was the first time I thought someone had it worse than me. Imagine that. I was getting fucked by almost anyone who would give my piece of shit a buck or two, and I felt like you had it worse."

Cas gets up and lifts his shirt, revealing the scars on his body. "Dec, I always knew my father didn't love me, that I was a bargaining chip, a piece of meat. I knew it every time he or someone he let fuck me would carve the memory on my flesh. But that day, the way she made me believe you were the bad one, the evil one and how she was good, helping you, I realized that no matter what kind of garbage my father was, he was honest about it. But that bitch was a piece of work. She's burning in your non-existent hell, not saving you from it."

Chapter 35

Cas

Fuck this motherfucker. I'm sick of his shit. I understand that he's trying for her, but fuck him. He should have begun his healing years ago.

My hand fidgets and I pull out a joint and light it.

Sunshine leans forward and clears her throat. "I'm not sure if pot is legal in France."

I sneer at her. "Like I give a shit. Didn't you hear? I've served hard time for killing a Catholic nun. You think a little French pig is going to frighten me?"

Sunshine appraises me. Her lips pull in a firm line, disappointment clear on her face. Well, she can get used to it. I'm not always gonna be her damn fuckin' circus clown. She nods as if washing her hands of me and turns back to Declan. She looks like she's hanging on his words. Guess the fucker has a good story.

Declan picks up his scotch and takes a long swig. "Well, it seems like Cas told you the brunt of it."

"I haven't told her shit. Why don't you tell her why you've got permanent holes in your hands? Or how you've got so many self-inflicted scars it scared a tattoo artist and he refused to work on your skin."

"That's rich coming from a guy who stabs himself to deal with his shit."

"Yes, but I don't pretend my imaginary daddy told me to."

"That's enough," Sunshine says sternly. "Religion isn't the issue here. God provides peace, hope, tranquility and it can take you out of isolation. God isn't the problem, abuse is. Declan isn't just going to abandon everything he knows because you and Lorne mock him. What you're doing isn't any better than what his aunt did."

I laugh bitterly. "You're right. She used to whip his back, and now I do. We're exactly the same. But, hey, all my father taught me was how to be violent and how to fuck. Seems you like that about me."

Noelle's head snaps back as if I've hit her.

I hate that she's staring at me like that. I hate that I've wounded her somehow, but I don't care. "Not a word I said was a lie. That's all I'm good for."

Before I can say another word, Noelle is on my lap. In my anger, I didn't even see her move, but as she wraps her arms around my neck, I feel a sense of peace. It's funny how one person can change your outlook with one simple touch. How being in their presence eases the bitterness. Noelle smiles, and all is right with the world.

Her fingers trail my flesh under my Nirvana T-shirt, brushing against my scars. "Why do you do it? Why do you cut?"

"It stops the voices in my head. Sometimes, it all gets too much. It's either a knife in my skin, or a bullet to my brain."

"Did you write all those words on your body?"

I grab her hand and lift my shirt. I guide her fingers along the words. The *Property of Sunshine* and the arrow below it. "The only ones I've ever carved are these."

"Who did the others?"

"My father. Some were punishments. Some were for money from people who had perverse desires."

"Why didn't you cover them up? You covered most of your upper body with tattoos." She gestures at my arms, hands, neck, and back. "Why did you leave such vile memories behind?"

I stare at her, her hand on my abdomen. "Because they're part of who I am. We can't run from our past. It's futile. Covering them would be like lying about who my father was, and I've lied enough for him. I wear the scars as a symbol of my survival. As a sign that we can overcome the most heinous acts and still thrive."

She glides her fingers from the words that give me joy to the ones that form my nightmares.

"Does anything help with the voice, other than cutting?"

I brush her hair back and glide my hand to her nape before crushing my mouth to hers. "You."

Chapter 36

Noelle

I've always been attracted to the broken. Not because I have a desire to fix them, more a need to love them. So it's fitting that I would be launched into the middle of three flawed, damaged, and battered men. Three men who have found a family with each other, even though they've never known one themselves. Their lives might be chaotic, dysfunctional, and violent, but their hearts, even while wrapped in a maze of thrones, are tender.

I rise from Cas's lap and pace the room, relieved we're the only ones in the restaurant. "I have a life here. I'm not willing to leave it."

Lorne leans back in his chair. "We'll move. I have a private jet. We can easily move back and forth between France and the U.S."

"You can't do anything without my consent."

Cas raises his arms. "I think I'm free of that." He points to Lorne and Declan. "It was these two who touched you that first night while you were passed out."

"Can we drug you with you permission?" Declan asks, his eyes cast down as if he's embarrassed for asking the question.

"Why do you want to drug me?"

Declan wrings his hands, not meeting my eyes. "It's easier. When you're asleep, it's easier."

"So you want to only fuck me when I'm sleeping?"

"I don't hurt you when you're not awake."

I approach him, placing my finger under his chin, and lift his face. I want him to look me in the eye, so I know he hears what I'm about to say. "You've never hurt me."

He grips my hips, hauling me to him. "That night, the night before you left. It was because of me."

"No! I left because of the whole situation. We went from zero to sixty. I needed time to process. But if you're worried about the sex, don't be. Apparently, I like it rough. What I don't like is being shut out, and not knowing who you are. That's what hurts me."

Goosebumps form on my arms as Declan trails his hands up them until he frames my face. Our foreheads touch and my breath hitches as he crushes his lips to mine. The kiss contradicts every other touch I've known from this man. It's not fevered or rough. There's no puncture from his teeth on my lips. No pain at my scalp from him pulling my hair. The kiss is soft, consumed with compassion, and wrapped in care. It begs for forgiveness and promises the world. This kiss is Declan's way of asking me to stay.

He pulls away from me, his steel-gray eyes searching mine. "So, drugging and fucking is on the table?"

I can't help smiling because Declan is. It's the first time he doesn't seem lost in pain. "If you go to therapy."

"Wait, what? Why do I have to go see a shrink?" He points to Cas and Lorne. "Do they have to? No way Cas will go. He'll get annoyed and kill the therapist."

"No, they don't. Only you."

"What if I say no?"

"Then I will too."

Declan traces my face with the pad of his finger as if trying to imprint on me through touch. "Well, I'm a lot of things, but not a liar."

The room spins and I yawn, desperate for my bed.

"I'll go to therapy, Eve."

Chapter 37

Declan

Above all, love each other deeply, because love covers over a multitude of sins.

I take in Noelle's naked sleeping body, lying on the bed. She'll need to have to love me fiercely if she wants to cover my sins.

This time it's different. This time she's ours.

"Who's ready to party?" Cas asks as he walks into the room carrying a giant tub of coconut oil.

Lorne pulls his head from Noelle's nipple. He's been sucking on it like a baby on its mother's tit for the past fifteen minutes. "What the hell is that for? We are going to fuck her, not cook her."

"You need lube, you idiot," Cas says, placing the tub on the nightstand. "You can't have three big cocks in that tiny cunt without a little extra help. And last I checked, no one here is under nine inches."

"Why do I have a feeling you've actually measured?"

Cas moves to the foot of the bed and pulls her legs apart. He brings his head up and licks. "Fucking delicious." He turns to me, his lips crimson with her blood. "Fuck, I can't wait to fuck this tight cunt."

Lorne gets on the bed and pulls Noelle on top of him. Holding her legs open.

Cas picks up the coconut oil from the nightstand and opens the lid. "I'm calling dibs on the cream pie."

His fingers glide into the container and he gathers the solidified oil in his hand before stepping up to me. "Be a man and fuck her like she deserves. Be here."

My eyes flutter shut, and I groan as his hands move up and down my hard cock, heating and liquifying the oil. The sensation is so overwhelming that I don't want him to stop, but I would rather cum in Noelle than all over Cas's hand.

Smooth leather around my neck. A belt, the buckle locked into place. My head is yanked back.

Cas's hot breath on my skin. "Gotta make sure you stay on a leash."

Love is patient, love is kind. It does not envy, it does not boast, it is not proud. It does not dishonor others, it is not self-seeking, it is not easily angered, it keeps no record of wrongs. Love does not delight in evil but rejoices with the truth. It always protects, always trusts, always hopes, always perseveres. Love never fails.

My hand moves to Cas's dick, and I tug, pulling his entire body closer to mine. Our cock heads glide against each other, building friction and need. "I've never told you, but you saved me. I thought it was Noelle who did, but it was you. You saved me, Lorne nurtured me, and she healed me."

Our eyes lock as we rub each other's dicks in silence. An unspoken understanding passes between us that only we fully comprehend. He yanks the belt, bringing my lips closer to his. A game he's playing, a taunt.

I bring my hand to the back of his dark brown hair and tug, never once taking my eyes off his. "You want to play chicken, Cas?"

He smiles at me, that goofy smile I love so much. The same one he gives when he's about to cause trouble. "You'd lose, Dec."

"Not this time, Caspian. This time I'm going to win." I crush my lips to his.

The tip of the belt grazes my side as Cas abandons my cock. His hands cradle my face, holding me tightly as if he's scared I might disappear if he lets go. He kisses with conviction, like I knew he would. Like he knows who he is, and he's proud of it. His kiss is a force, a volcano that's been simmering for so long until it erupts.

His fists my hair, pulling my head back. "Fucking finally. I've waited a long time for that."

"I know."

"Enough of this sappy shit. We've got some prime pussy to plow."

I roll my eyes and turn back to Eve. Lorne's snuggled in her sweet pussy, holding her legs wide open for us. Cas dips his hand in coconut oil and slathers it around Lorne's dick as he moves in and out of her in rapid succession. "Where did you get a tub that big?"

Cas doesn't look at me as he moves his hand along Lorne's cock to the entrance of Noelle's pussy. "Costco."

"Lube at the pharmacy wasn't good enough?"

"They were tiny tubes." He points at his crotch. "We're packing. Usually, I'd be all for ripping her apart and feasting on the blood, but I'd rather her be conscious."

Cas reaches out with his other hand and pulls me by the dick. He doesn't say a word as he wraps his mouth around my cock and takes me all the way to the back of his throat. I grip his hair as I thrust to get even further. But this time the blow job is different. It's not an animalistic urge to satiate a sinful need within me. It's something more. Is this how people feel when they finally accept Christ, like they've unlocked a truth that shall set them free? Because right now, with his tongue swirling around my dick, I might be born again.

He pulls me out of his mouth and smiles before rising to his feet. He grips my throat and moves closer, pulling me toward Noelle's sleeping body and guiding my cock toward her entrance. I thrust forward and glide along Lorne's cock until I'm nestled next to him.

"Fuck," Lorne groans. "She's so fucking tight with both of us in there."

"She's about to be stuffed," Cas says before pushing the tip of his cock inside her.

Cas continues to smear coconut oil, lubricating her tight cunt. He pushes his dick slowly into her entrance. Gripping the leather strap of the belt, he pulls me to him. I part my lips, longing for another kiss. He spits in my mouth before tugging my bottom lip between his teeth. "We're fucking her Dec. All three of us and her. She's the body of Christ, Dec. She's everything holy." He pulls my hair back, and my blood trickles from his lips. "This is perfect. Our cocks side by side inside fucking paradise."

Lorne stiffens, holding her still as he cums in her. He slowly pulls out, brushing against our cocks. Cas and I stare down at her pussy as some of his cum leaks onto our cocks.

"Fuck," Cas grunts. "That's going to taste so fucking good." He dips his finger to where we're joined and scoops a dollop onto his finger before offering it to me. "Be a good boy and open wide."

My mouth falls open and I suck Lorne's cum off Cas's finger. His mouth clasps to mine and our tongues intertwine as we fuck our girl and explode in unison.

Lorne is on his knees with our semi hard cocks in his hands. His velvet tongue rotates between cleaning Cas's dick and mine. He looks at us. "You recorded everything, right?"

Cas points to the Camera in the room's corner. "Sure did. Even zoomed in on the bed."

Chapter 38

Noelle

Strong arms hold me still. I force my eyes to open.

Declan.

I'm in his arms, and his chin rests on the crown of my head. My hand moves to my throat on instinct.

"Relax, Eve. You're safe," he says, his deep voice soothing.

Grunting sounds come from the screen. I turn my head and gasp in shock. There, on the forty-two-inch monitor hanging on the wall, is graphic porn. Three guys and a girl. They're all fucking her. The two men move slightly. Oh. My. God. That's me. I'm lying on a bed while all three guys fuck me and cum is leaking from my pussy. So much cum.

The movie stops and I turn to Declan, but before I say anything, there's a new scene. It's me again, with Cas's head between my parted legs. My stomach rolls and breasts are on display as he grips my thighs. I look wanton and sexy. My reaction shocks me.

Slurping sounds from Cas licking the cum overpower the room and then the camera zooms in to show the cum covering his lips oozing from my center.

He lifts his head and smiles at the camera. His face is covered in cum and blood. He looks whimsical and homicidal. "I'm gonna have this for dessert every night for the rest of my life."

Epilogue

Noelle (Two Years Later)

There's something both dangerous and safe about the forest. As I stand here, surrounded by the tall elms, evergreens and ferns, I'm reminded of the massive world and my insignificance within it.

I shut my eyes and take in a deep breath before the rustling of the fall leaves alert me to the fact that I'm not alone. The element of danger peering around every corner.

Another snap. This time a twig. As the sounds get closer and closer, I do the only thing I can; I run.

Two powerful arms grab my waist and hoist me in the air as I peer behind me. I turn my face and Cas is smirking at me. I still don't know how these men can lift me, as if I weigh nothing more than a nine-pound baby.

"Where are you running off to, Sunshine?"

My foot kicks out, and I nail him in the shin. He immediately drops me and swears profanities. I fight the urge to make sure he's okay, but I also know that's not part of the game. The hunt is on. So, once again, I run.

I make it a few steps before an arm wraps around my throat and I'm slammed down on the forest floor.

"You had a good run, Snow, but you already know that the big bad wolves always catch their prey."

I squint my eyes and glare up at three pairs of predatory eyes. Green, blue and gray. "Did you have to slam me so damn hard? I'm going to have bruises all along my back."

Declan bends down, gripping my hair with such strength that I'm forced to move where he wants. "Sweet Eve, bruises on your back won't be the only thing you're worried about. I haven't been able to fuck you for eight weeks."

I'm on my knees, peering up at their naked forms. Declan releases my hair and unzips his pants, revealing his cock. There, on over nine inches of rock hard cock, is Declan's new piercing. A collection of Frenum piercings all lined up in a row appearing like a ladder.

"I tried it out already , Sunshine. It's like going from a Honda to a Ferrari."

I glare at Cas, a little envious that he got to sample the goods before me. So envious that I bolt.

"Oh, little Eve, you're in for it now."

Joy bubbles within me as I run past the tree, the three men I love more than anything hot at my heels.

I'm just about to reach the clearing when an arm wraps around my shoulder and pulls me back into the woods, pushing me up against a tree. "Where do you think you're going, my pretty little slut? We're not finished playing with you yet."

I'm about to speak when I'm rendered speechless by Lorne's fingers invading my pussy. "Such a good girl. Always, so wet and ready for us."

He grips my throat and pushes me down to the ground before slapping my face with his cock. "Open wide, Sis."

My mouth opens on his command and he glides his cock along my lips. A merciless tease. I lean forward to capture him in my mouth, but he steps back, slapping me in the face with the head of his dick. "Such a perfect whore. You want your big brother's cock, don't you, my pretty little slut?"

"Yes," I plead.

Lorne smiles and backs away. "Let me see you crawl in the dirt, like a pathetic whore. Show me how badly you want to choke on your brother's dick."

The thrill of the degrading act fuels me. With my hands and knees grounded in the dirt, I move one limb at a time until I'm in front of his cock. Lips parted and panting for a taste.

Lorne laughs as he bends down. "Such a good girl. You ready for your big brother to give you a tasty treat?"

Dampness floods my center with every demeaning act. I nod my head and his jaw ticks. The humor is gone, replaced by something else; something darker. He grips my hair, tugging my head back, and spits directly in my open and waiting mouth. "What did I tell you about nodding, Snow?"

When I don't answer, he yanks my hair harder. "I asked you a question, little sister. You ready for your big brother to give you a treat?."

"Yes. P-please choke me with your thick cock."

He pulls my head back, standing over me, his balls resting on my chin. His firm grip holds onto my neck as he dips his cock into my mouth and hits the back of my throat.

The gagging sounds coming from my mouth are the only sounds I can focus on. Lorne is being so vicious that I think I might choke on either this large member or my spit. His balls slap down on my skin as his cock punctures my uvula. He's not holding back and I don't want him to.

I love the sweet moments with my men. However, these moments when they're unhinged, free of any decorum and liberated from their cages are my favorite. They allow me to see the darkness, giving me a way to be a part of their true selves. With every hard thrust, bruise and bite, I know they are mine and I'm theirs, wholly.

"Look at you Sunshine," Cas says as he lifts my legs in the air, "such a good little slut sucking your big brother's cock. Now let's see how well that tight cunt of yours can take your daddy's dick."

The crown of my head is on the forest floor. Lorne is straddling my neck, his dick pushing further in my mouth. My ass lifts off the ground as Cas pounds into me. His thrusts are wild and untamed, just like he is. Cas, my sweet dark angel. A man who relishes chopping off a head in the morning and rubbing my feet at night. In many ways, he's the sweetest out of my three loves. His sweetness, though wrapped up in brutality, is one of the most endearing things about him.

I moan on Lorne's cock as Cas rubs my clit. "You're going to be a good girl and cum all over Daddy's cock, aren't you Sunshine?"

I mumble a yes and Lorne's dick twitches in my mouth.

"Such a dirty slut, Snow. You're such a filthy whore," Lorne says before Declan grabs his throat and squeezes. A heightened sense of fear pounds through my body with the realization that Lorne no longer has control. Declan does.

"Fuck her mouth, Lorne. Show her the glory of your love."

Lorne's face turns red. His mouth opening for tiny gasps of breath. His eyes roll back and his body stiffens before hot, salty cum sprays down my throat.

Cum and spit fall out from the sides of my lips as Lorne's body slumps over and he gasps for breath.

'Why is it hot watching you almost die," Cas asks.

'Because," Lorne wheezes, "a part of you gets hard at the sight of death."

Cas tilts his head as if contemplating before smirking and nodding his head. "This is true. I'd probably kill all you motherfuckers to get off if I didn't love you so much."

I burst out laughing, cum and spit now covering my face.

Then a groan escapes from Cas. I turn my head to see that Declan has a knife in his hand and there's blood trickling from Cas' chest. "Fuck. Cut her. I want blood on my whore when I dump into her sweet cunt."

Declan smiles, but all I can do is stare at his rock hard cock and the line of metal that now adorns it.

He smirks and glides the tip of the blade between my breasts and nicks me along my right nipple. "Wanna try the hardware, don't you, slut?"

"Yes," I moan.

Cas lifts me up, dipping me at my back as he grips my nipple between his lips and sucks the blood that flows from there. The sensation of his cock and his teeth on my nipple is too much. I grip his arms and scream, throwing my legs around his waist and jumping on his dick to quicken my release. "Fuck me, Cas. Fuck my tight pussy. I want to cream all over your thick cock. Tear me apart."

"That's it my little slut, show Daddy how badly you want his baby batter."

With my arms around his neck and his powerful arms supporting me, I bounce on him and cum in waves. But I'm not allowed to come down from them. The bark of the tree scrapes at my back as Cas jack hammers into me. His sharp teeth are on my shoulders as he tears into my flesh. "I'm gonna fill this tight pussy of ours with so much cum. I want to see it leaking out of you. Dripping down your thick thighs. I'm going to rub it into your round sexy belly and watch as it jiggles for me, just like your juicy tits. I'm going to make you crawl for Daddy just so I can watch it leak from your ass. Then I'm going to force your face on the floor alongside mine and we'll clean it up together."

That's when I scream again, coming again just from his filthy mouth. "I'm coming, Cas. I'm coming."

"That's a good little slut. Always giving Daddy that hot pussy juice."

With a vicious groan, Cas goes lax and roars his release.

Before I can even catch my breath, Declan replaces Cas. The piercings on his shaft are brief explosions in my pussy with every rung he pushes inside of me.

He brings his head down to my neck, "know why I got this piercing?"

"No," I pant as my hands grip his shoulders and my nails dig in. "But I'm not complaining."

Shivers glide along my body when he laughs. "I was in exile my entire life, always wanting to find home. No matter how hard I would try to climb out of despair, I would always stumble and fall. Until you. You're my Jacob's Ladder. You're the dream that saved me."

My heart constricts as tears fall down my face. My beautiful Declan.

I close my eyes and get lost in his rapture, and surrender to the bliss.

"How full of awe is this place! This is none other than the house of God, and this is the gate of heaven. Lorne was right. You're the key to paradise."

And with poetry on his lips, he fucks me into oblivion.

The next book in the Darkly Ever After Series is

Briar's book. A dark Why Choose reimagining of Sleeping Beauty called In Dreams. You can pre-order Here

Stay Connected

Website
Amazon
TikTok
Facebook
Instagram
GoodReads

Printed in Great Britain
by Amazon

47619854R00129